Roger Tapley has spent his life living in schools as a teacher and a headteacher. He loves telling stories to anyone that prepares to listen. Now retired, he spends his time in daily walks and jumping into his Morgan classic car and driving with the roof down across the Kent countryside gives him the ideas for his stories.

This is for you, Alyssa, my very brave granddaughter suffering from Leukaemia. Proceeds for the sale of this book donated to Ward 27, Teenage Cancer Trust Unit at Leicester Royal Infirmary.

Roger Tapley

THE COTTAGE OF SECRETS

AUSTIN MACAULEY PUBLISHERS™

LONDON • CAMBRIDGE • NEW YORK • SHARJAH

A CIP catalogue record for this title is available from the British Library.

ISBN 9781398428287 (Paperback)
ISBN 9781398428294 (Hardback)
ISBN 9781398428300 (ePub e-book)

www.austinmacauley.com

First Published 2022
Austin Macauley Publishers Ltd®
1 Canada Square
Canary Wharf
London
E14 5AA

To Alyssa and Liam, thank you for your ideas that have helped in writing this story.

To James, my son, for finding the time to present lively illustrations that improve the text despite his busy work schedule.

To all children who love to read or listen to stories I am always thinking about you when I write my books.

Chiavala (Lad)

Liam sat on the sofa, he was bored and it was only the second day of the holiday. Alyssa had gone to a party! She was always going to parties or 'sleep overs'. Only this party was a small one with three girls and they were not going anywhere. Just playing music and talking about boys! How boring was that! He was going to see Jax, his best mate, to ride his new bike and play in his large garden. It was as big as a football pitch. You could get lost amongst the trees and bushes. They had made their own den in a very secret part of the garden at a point farthest away from the house! The last time he went he was sure he saw strange species of animals lurking in the trees. But Jax said it was the wind blowing the branches! Liam had a vivid imagination. He was well known for the strange stories he told at school, not many people believed what he had to say! His mum told him to stop dreaming and get on with his homework, just like his teachers! He felt like a prisoner, chained to a dungeon floor, gagged with that silver sticky tape that hurt when it was ripped off his face! Suddenly the phone rang.

"Liam, can you answer that?" His mother was a teacher and was always working on school projects and stuff. Liam wearily walked over to the phone. It looked like phones used in the 1960s. The phone was slowly moving across the hall table. Liam just stared at it, would it fall off? He was sure there was a hidden hand slowly pushing it.

"Liam did you hear me?" his mum shouted. "Oh for goodness sake, never mind." She rushed down the stairs grabbing the phone, nearly ripping the cord out of its socket.

Liam went and sat back down on the sofa. His mum quickly finished the conversation and came into the lounge-like a battleship rocking about in a rough sea. "That was Jax's mum; he has fallen off his new bike and they are taking him to the hospital for a check-up, you will not be going out to his house today."

"Do you think they will let me borrow the bike, Mum? He cannot ride a bike with a broken leg."

Jenny Durtnall frowned. "Liam, that's not a nice thought. Anyway, the bike might have been damaged. Why don't you do something useful?"

"Yeah, I get it! Tidy my room. Clean out the stick insect cage," he interrupted and went upstairs to get dressed.

Liam glanced over at the mountain of toys he had deposited in the middle of his bedroom floor. Captain America. The iron patriot. Spider-Man and Doc Ock's tentacle trap. He started swapping heads and arms to make his favourite creation. Captain Patriot looked great with Spider-Man's head and the cannon blaster and shield on his back taken from Patriot's body. This could be used as a vicious Frisbee. Thrown to maim and cut off the hands and feet of his attacker. Liam's mind raced into the scene, picturing the blood gushing from heads and hands as the blade cut into flesh and bone. But he was having trouble getting the missile launcher to work so fire power was low. There were too many attackers to deal with all at once.

"*Shut the door*," he shouted, throwing the toy on the floor. He was frustrated. This was a phrase he always used to stop his mind sending him into dark places. Nothing else seemed to grab his imagination today! He had to be somewhere new and exciting for his mind to grow. For him to feel alive. To feel 'Mega'. That's what his group of friends at school called it. Whether it was jumping backwards off the high wall in the playground or sneaking off into the copse just off the playground to find 'stingers' they could pick up without being stung. He started to panic, his mum would find him a task which he would hate if he did not do something soon.

"Hey, Mum, I am going out!" Liam shouted, leaving his toys in an untidy pile on his bedroom carpet.

His parents' ideas of bringing up children were unusual. Liam and Alyssa were encouraged to go out together on their own and look after themselves. They had been left in places near home and were told to find their way back. The older they became the greater the challenge. When Dad was not working, he was often thinking of more adventures. He was building a climbing tower in the back garden. It was fifteen feet high and had three sections to it. Once the children had managed to climb each tower, he would then take some support pegs away moving the towers further apart. This meant to get from one tower to another they had to fling themselves out towards the next one and grab for the supporting rail. Their garden was an exciting place but their friends were not allowed to visit because they returned to their houses bruised and with dirty clothes.

The front door slammed as Liam rushed out the door.

"Be back for lunch. Have you got your watch with you?" Jenny Durtnall looked out of the window as she saw Liam slouching down the drive. Even at eight years of age, he was beginning to walk like a teenager! Looking down at the ground, shoulders poking forward, staring at his feet. She hoped he was not too upset about his cancelled day out with Jax. She felt a bit guilty about shouting at him earlier. Sometimes this teaching job took too much of her time away from the children. At times like this, she began to regret changing her job to train as a teacher at a lower wage when compared to working for the Otis Lift company.

"Always in a rush to go nowhere!" muttered Jenny, chewing on a pencil and stumbling back to her desk to complete another scheme of work for next term. She paused and thought it would have been nice to have gone out with Liam today. Sometimes, she hated her job!

Liam lived in a house on the edge of a small village estate near a large ancient woodland that could be traced back to the 13th century going as far back as the Doomsday Book. Liam loved wandering amongst the old oak trees, looking up into the branches that seemed to soar up to reach the clouds. He thought of them as tree rockets, and had attempted to climb many of them, he had fallen off most of those he tried to climb. The taller and narrower birch trees were too thick with foliage to climb, so he left these alone. Copses of hazel undergrowth were great for collecting 'lambs tails', the male catkins, which hung on their flimsy stems and looked very much to Liam like 'hanged men' waiting to be cut down from the scaffold. Liam's dad being a member of the Woodland Trust knew a great deal about what was happening there. Due to species such as the western hemlock, and western cedar tree which gave out heavy shade, meant the old oak trees were finding it difficult to survive.

Liam was thinking of going down to the wood after listening to his father discussing the recent arrival of a gypsy community. They were not popular with the villagers because of the damage they would cause to the wood with all of their cars and caravans. Plans were being made by the local community in supporting the woodland trust to get rid of them. Liam thought he would go and see what was going on.

As he was walking down the lane leading to the woods, he saw a cat precariously balancing on an overhanging branch. It fell off onto the path just in front of him.

"Hi beautiful, I see you like trees as much as I do." He bent down to tickle the cat under its chin. It had a dark smoky face with a blue colour inside its ears and a beige and white coat. The most striking part were the green eyes. An unusual colour for a Siamese cat whose eyes were usually blue. The creature rubbed itself against Liam's legs making it difficult for him to walk. He stopped to have a better look at its collar which had its name on it. 'Snickitylickers'. There was a small bell hanging from the collar under the cat's chin. "Hey, what an unusual name for a cat? I bet people call you lickers." Liam paused and quickly turned around to see if anyone was listening to him talking to a cat. There was nobody about, *a lucky escape*, he thought. As he continued down to the woods, he noticed the cat was following him. The quiet tinkle of the bell made an eerie sound. He imagined being followed by an alien with an axe or some form of heavy weapon. *"Shut the door,"* he whispered and the scene disappeared. Suddenly the cat ran past him making for the path into the woods. Liam saw the gypsy encampment, having listened to some of his friends' parents talking about how messy gipsies were, he felt nervous. Gipsies were a bunch of thieves, dirty, untidy. His father did not agree, he had one friend who was a traveller, with a rich Romany heritage, Tom Loveridge.

"Oh no," he gasped as he saw the cat jump over the gate suddenly sitting down to wash itself and giving him that stare to say 'come in'.

"I don't think I want to go in there!" he muttered. It was the gypsy encampment.

"Hello, what are you staring at?" The boy was similar in height to Liam, black hair with a tanned but spotty face which reminded Liam of a pirate.

"*Shut the door,*" whispered Liam to stop the thought taking him into his more creative world. He was well built; had muscular arms. He knew he looked powerful by the way he sauntered up to the gate. The most striking thing about him was his eyes that were green just like the cat. He was also dressed in a funny way, like a peasant, with a waistcoat tied up with string covering a large fluffy looking shirt with large cuffs and trousers that stopped at the knees. He was wearing a pair of brown boots.

"Oh, I was just going for a walk in the woods and stopped to look at your place," Liam answered in a voice that hopefully did not show how nervous he felt.

The boy who was chewing a blade of grass spat it out. "Do you live in the village? I am sure I have seen you before?"

"Yes, just around the corner from here." Feeling uncomfortable, Liam looked down at his shoes to avoid those staring eyes. This guy seemed very confident.

"You're trespassing! Better get out of here before I come over the gate to move you on." Quickly, the boy bent down and picked up a large stone and started throwing it up and catching it in his hand. "I consider villagers as my enemies!" he replied.

Although feeling nervous, Liam was beginning to feel angry. "I have every right to walk through that gate and into these woods as this is a public right of way!"

"OK, I will give you five seconds!" Jumping on top of the gate getting ready to aim the rock at Liam's head, the boy started counting. "One, two…"

A dark-haired girl came running up to the gate, her long black hair streaming out behind her. She was wearing a corset styled front and a long green and burgundy full-length dress. It had a shaped neckline and cuffed sleeves like her brother.

"Hey," she shouted, "don't you dare, pig brain!" She thumped the boy in the back and sent him flying over the gate. He dropped the rock and rolled in an untidy heap onto the grass in front of Liam's feet. He quickly got up glaring at the girl and brushing the dirt off his scuffed knees. The girl opened the gate. "Come in," she said brushing some of that long black hair out of her eyes. "I heard him shouting at you." She glared at the boy who immediately took a hurried step backwards as she clouted him around the head. He did not have much to say and Liam thought that he did not look powerful anymore.

Liam followed both children into the gypsy encampment looking rather nervous. The children introduced themselves. The boy's name was Jal and his elder sister was called Rawnie. Liam noticed Jal was not that keen on shaking his hand and he was still holding the stone he was intending to throw at Liam before his sister stopped him.

"What's wrong with him then? Why is he so unfriendly?"

"He gets like that. It's because everywhere we go people seem to pick on us and call us names. I always have to watch him to keep him out of trouble."

"Is that your cat?" Liam noticed the cat was still walking about near them and rubbing herself up against Rawnie's legs. "She wanted me to come here for some reason."

Rawnie picked the cat up and gave her a cuddle. "No, she does not belong to us but she is often on the site as our granny keeps feeding her with kippers."

"She kept following me as I walked down to the woods."

Jal and Rawnie kept glancing at each other as if Liam had discovered a secret that they shared and did not want him to know. Rawnie did most of the talking as they walked around the site. Their parents both worked. But they did not explain what they did. They just laughed when asked. Liam explained that he wanted to know what gypsies did.

Jal suddenly grabbed Liam's shirt. "Don't call us gypsy, we are Romany and proud of our heritage!"

"Calm down, Jal!" She turned to Liam and explained some of the history of their race. They had been persecuted throughout history. Four out of five Roma and traveller people had experienced a 'hate crime'. Rawnie explained that the term 'Gypsy' was understood to be a 'hate' word and this is why her brother was upset. "Come and see our wagon," she said.

"Don't you mean caravan?" But when Liam saw it looked like an old-fashioned wagon that was used many years ago and was pulled by horses. He was amazed at how small and colourful it was.

The Romany camp was small with only two wagons. Just behind the children's wagon was an even bigger one. He was told this was The Burton. A caravan used by fairground travellers. It had angel lamps, wooden carvings of flowers, snakes and what looked like a green woodpecker on the front door. It was festooned with flowers. Fuchsias in pots draped over gutters and hanging baskets of bougainvillea swaying in the breeze. There were two Irish Cobb horses grazing near the wagons. They had a black and white mottled coat with pink-skinned patches around the head, neck and chest. They were very friendly and loved being patted and fed grass. As the children walked past, a crotchety old woman grasping a walking stick stuck her head out of the window.

"Hey, who's that wiv' yer, Rawnie?"

"Hi Gran, we are just showing a friend around the site." She whispered to Liam. "That's granny Pat whatever you do, don't mention the word 'gypsy' she will go 'ape' just like Jal!"

"Bring him! Like to see new people! I am too old to travel far these days!" grumbled the old woman.

Rawnie whispered to Liam. "She speaks funny because she has no teeth!"

Granny Pat reminded Liam of an oversized guinea pig with a yellowish face, whiskers that seemed to sprout out of her ears, a chin and eyebrows that looked like table mats. The children all walked up the steps to enter the caravan. Liam gasped as this caravan was even more luxurious than the other one. It reminded him of a caravan he saw at a funfair that came to his village last year. There were cabinets on the walls displaying rosette ribbons dated 1841, two parakeets in cages and a fish tank containing some very strange creatures which

Liam had not seen before. His dad had a fish tank in the lounge with Catfish, Gourami and Angelfish, these creatures did not look anything like tropical fish. More like worms with eyes on stalks. Liam's mind began to race as he felt himself being drawn into the tank but managed to stop himself by thinking '*shut the door*'. There were also no bubbles coming out of the tank which meant it did not have an aeration pump attached. So how did these creatures survive? There was a cast-iron stove used for cooking. The main room was made out of wood with a ceiling showing colours and pictures of exotic plants. Behind the sliding doors, at the back, was a raised double bed with a smaller berth for children below. The children explained this was a Burton Wagon, it was originally undecorated and could only be taken on smooth roads due to its small wheels. Their parents had bought and decorated these themselves and then had given it to Granny Pat.

"Stranger," the parakeets chorused sticking their heads out and strutting around the cage.

Granny Pat stared at Liam, she pointed a gnarled old finger at his face. Then slowly beckoned him closer. Jal pushed Liam forward and he nearly tripped into her but just managed to keep his balance. She smelt damp like the lavender plants in his garden at home. His mum said lavender kept the wasps away in the hot weather and there were certainly no wasps in the wagon, so it seemed to have worked. He was grabbed by the shoulder as the old lady put both hands around him giving him a squeeze. "Ah!" The old woman groaned. "Some good bones on him, even though he looks like a stick insect," she cackled.

Liam thought about his stick insects at home, when they moved they seemed to wobble. There was no way he resembled one of those! Last week he had been awarded a white belt in Taekwondo. This made him cross, very angry. Before he could stop himself he pushed the old woman away and shouted, "I am not going to be insulted or frightened by you. How dare you call me names!"

Both Jal and Rawnie glanced at each other and Jal looked ready to run out the door. Rawnie grabbed Liam's arm, thinking he might also be thinking of running for his life. The old lady smiled showing her red gums and started laughing while licking her lips with a tongue that looked a very peculiar colour.

"This one has a bit o fight in him. He'll do! Welcome to me home!" She glanced at her grandchildren, nodding her head. "He'll make a good messenger for us to get justice!" she muttered.

Liam looked confused and glanced at Rawnie who sighed and raised her eyebrows as she mouthed, "She's a bit stupid."

The children were given tea and biscuits which looked a bit strange but tasted very nice. The old lady laughed a great deal when questioned and she was very good at not providing answers. She paused, turned around to grab a china pipe, and filled it with tobacco. Rawnie picked up a box of matches and helped her light it. Granny Pat started puffing the smoke out of her mouth in the shape of 'o' rings, which reminded Liam of scenes in some Indian movies, puffing the pipe of peace. His mind started to wander but he quickly shut the door on his imagination.

"Your job, young man, is to seek justice and honour for the sake of our destiny." She paused and stared at him. "Aye, destiny 'young'un' remember this! Forget this at your peril!"

She coughed out a laugh. "Destiny, truth, justice, honour, that will take us home." She kept repeating these words over and over again in the form of a mantra. The words seemed to hypnotise Liam whose eyes started glazing over.

Snickitylickers suddenly jumped in through the window and came and sat in the middle of the room staring quite fiercely at granny Pat. The old lady seemed to get a bit nervous. "Ah right! 'Bout time you were going then. Enjoy our site and come back soon, eh? For more of those 'biscuits'."

"Bye Gran!" shouted the children as they grabbed Liam pulling him roughly out of the door and down the steps.

"Get off me, will you?" shouted Liam rubbing his shoulder. "What's the hurry?"

Granny Pat answered his question by shouting out that her grandchildren had to be back by noon to do 'the chores'.

"What were those creatures in the fish tank? Why did your gran look afraid of the cat? Why was she talking about honour and destiny?" The children were dressed in strange things making them look like children from another age. Their granny was the same. "Why are you dressed like that?" he said.

"It's a joke, that's all," replied Rawnie glancing quickly at her brother who nodded his head to show he agreed with his sister. "We are going to be interviewed today by the local paper, and we want to show them our traveller heritage. The more people know about us the better it will be!"

For the next hour, the children walked around the site playing on the adventure playground that the Romany families had recently built. Unfortunately, they had cleared some of the hazel-copses to do this. There was a wooden castle with a moat, and two treehouses.

"Come on city boy race you to the top of this treehouse," Jal dashed off with Liam running fast to keep up with him. He managed to push Jal over, then jumped and grabbed the ladder climbing quickly to the top.

Rawnie sat on the fence shouting out rude messages, calling Liam a wimp, or a wobbly stick insect. She was quick to notice what irritated him, but this only made him more determined to keep ahead of Jal. Also, he did not mind being teased by such a pretty girl. His recent experiences with his dad's climbing tower had helped him and had shown Jal that he was somebody prepared to take risks. The boys collapsed onto the top floor gasping for air. Liam's legs were screaming in agony and he groaned as he fell into the treehouse with Jal on top of him. It was impossible for him to move.

"Time for your initiation test, dog's breath, earthy boy!"

"Filthy gypsy," spat Liam feeling much more confident in challenging Jal now that he matched his speed in climbing up the treehouse. This made Jal pause to think of a more insulting response, and Liam took this opportunity to arch his back in an attempt to throw the boy over the edge of the treehouse into the canopy of trees below. However, he was not strong enough and this only made Jal giggle and smile. He leant back and took out of his back pocket what Liam thought to be a piece of metal. He held it in front of Liam's face as it glinted in the sun. He pressed a button on the side and out flicked a blade.

"This is 'Scimitar' my tool for making badges out of skin. Are you ready to be cut!"

Now, this was quite a worrying situation, thought Liam. "You cut me with your little pen knife, fancy boy and I will return here with my gang and return the favour!"

"Threats won't stop me punishing you for calling me a gypsy, little Liam." Jal was laughing as he raised the knife. "Hold out your left hand!"

At that moment, Snickitylickers with a howl jumped out of the branches of a nearby tree landing on Jarl's shoulders. She had followed the boys in their race to the top of the treehouse. Jal let out a scream as the cat dug its paws into his skin. The cat arched its back and hissed.

"I'm sorry, I'm sorry!" whimpered Jal rubbing his damaged shoulder that was now beginning to bleed. Without a sound, Snickitylickers leapt into the trees and the two boys were left confronting each other. Jal held out his left hand and Liam saw a scar in the shape of a triangle with a cross inside it. Just below his thumb joint. "That Liam is my badge of honour. To show I am Romany!"

"But Snickitylickers does not think you deserve it yet!" muttered Liam.

Both boys climbed down as Rawnie was yelling it was nearly 12 o'clock and they had to start work. Both ran off, back to the settlement, leaving Liam on his own. As he was wandering back to the front gate he noticed the cat close behind him. Liam bent down to stroke her. "OK I get the message. I must go. Thanks for helping me with Jal." As he walked home he thought there were a lot of mysteries for him to solve. Why were Granny Pat and the children afraid of the cat? Why was the cat protecting him from Jal? The badge of honour; what did this mean and why was he led to the Romany Settlement? In just over a week they had invaded the woodland and built a very impressive adventure playground with a treehouse, and a castle with a moat that actually had water in it? This looked like developing into an adventure and it certainly was better than playing with his tablet and with his superheroes in his bedroom!

Chey (Girl)

Alyssa swung around and around to the music; her pink party
dress swirled out nearly knocking over Jasmine's new make-

up case which had been left on the table. It was Jasmine's birthday present from Alyssa but Jasmine had not been impressed.

"Oh thank you sooo much, Lissy it is the same colour as my other one!" She ripped the present out of the wrapping paper throwing it on the carpet then picked it up and started to criticise its quality. "Hmm! The hinges on the lid look a bit weak, darling! Where did you buy it? Was it a bargain basement purchase?"

This made Alyssa angry. When they went shopping the other day, Jasmine had picked up the case and told Alyssa she would like it for her birthday! Jasmine knew that Alyssa hated being called Lissy.

"Well! If you remember when we went out shopping the other day, you did tell me you liked it! It was not worth buying you something expensive as you are so clumsy."

Jasmine walked off with Jess into the garden after putting some music on the CD player in the lounge. She left Alyssa to dance on her own. Alyssa did not want to chase after her so she stayed in the lounge and danced on her own. After a while, she felt a bit foolish and went into the garden to find the other two girls. She immediately saw them hiding behind the silver birch tree. As she ran over to them, she heard them giggling. "Why don't you both grow up and stop being so childish!" she said, standing in the middle of the lawn with her hands on her hips.

"Hey Jess," shouted Jasmine, "she reminds me of old witchity grub!" This was the nickname they gave their science teacher at school. A rather pompous lady with a double chin that quivered when she spoke. The woman was always muttering to herself during the lessons and when it was time to finish the lesson she had a habit of calling the pupils 'my caterpillars'.

"Grubby Lissy, grubby Lissy!" chanted Jasmine glancing over at Jess and glaring at her to join in with the chant. Jess who had been very quiet up to then looked uncomfortable. Jasmine grabbed Jess by the arm and both girls started running. Jasmine ran through one of the flower beds, picked up some wet mud and threw it staining Alyssa's new dress. Alyssa suddenly felt very cold. She just stood there clenching her hands tightly together looking down at the brown muddy stain that was dribbling down her chest. It would not have been so bad if she had worn a darker colour to hide the stain. She knew why Jasmine was acting in this way. She had started seeing Toby at the weekends from school, and Jasmine liked Toby as well, but he now seemed more interested in going out with Alyssa. Last week they went ten pin bowling together and had a picnic in the park. She had even invited Jasmine on both of these occasions as she did not want to upset her. But Jasmine had not been allowed to go. Her parents did not like her going out with Alyssa on her own. When shopping in Leicester, Jasmine's mum had to be there as well. So this made matters worse. It was, therefore, a surprise that Jasmine had invited Alyssa over to the party and to the 'sleepover'.

Alyssa brushed off most of the dirt and then realised the reason for being invited to the party had given Jasmine an opportunity to get her own back. *I will not retaliate*, she thought, *that will only make matters worse*. She slowly walked back into the house and sat down on the carpet in the lounge. One of her favourite tracks. 'What doesn't kill you, makes you stronger' by Kelly Clarkson. *Yes,* thought Alyssa, *I shall be strong after all I am nearly a mature woman.*

The other girls dashed into the lounge still giggling. They were all called into the dining room for the birthday meal. It was getting late. Jasmine's dad came in with a dishcloth in his hand. "Well, girlies that's the washing up done. I don't understand how three people can make such a mess when sitting down to a meal! Now time for bed, we have put two sleeping bags in Jasmine's room as I don't think she will be happy to give up her bed, will you sweetheart?"

Jasmine gave her father a beatific smile. "I don't mind, Daddy. I want my friends to be comfortable."

Her father suddenly noticed Alyssa's dress. "What happened to you, Alyssa?"

Alyssa glanced at Jasmine who was looking rather worried about getting the blame. "Oh, I tripped over in the garden, Mr Chambers. I am afraid I am a bit clumsy at times!" She could see the relief on Jasmine's face. *I hope that will stop us from arguing now*, she thought.

"Once you are ready for bed, my wife will put your dress in the washing machine. We don't want you getting into trouble when you get home!" He laughed.

"No, Dad," simpered Jasmine, "she can be such a clumsy clown!"

Don't push it, girl, thought Alyssa giving Jasmine one of her evil stares.

The girls went upstairs accompanied by Ruffie, Jasmine's pet wire-haired terrier. He made a great fuss of the two guests running around the bedroom, barking and nipping ankles. "Ouch," shouted Jess, rubbing her legs. She wasn't that keen on dogs. They did not seem to like her. Alyssa didn't mind and instead of jumping on the bed to join Jess to get out of the dogs' way, she squatted on the floor and put her arms out.

Ruffie was delighted and immediately rolled over onto his back to have his tummy tickled.

"How gross," shouted Jess but seeing the look on Jasmine's face having criticised her pet decided not to say anything more.

"OK," said Jasmine, "who wants the bed?"

"I will have it!" Jess quickly replied. "I am not allowed to sleep low down on the floor because of my asthma."

Jasmine raised her eyebrows in disbelief. "Since when have you had asthma? Don't lie! Never seen you out of breath in my life."

"Did not stop you running around the garden this evening." Jasmine grabbed Jess and pushed her off the bed and like a frightened imp, Jess pushed herself into a corner grabbing a pillow to hide her face.

"It's true," she cried.

Jasmine calmly came and sat next to her friend. "Calm down, sweetie pie! If you really want the bed you have to earn it. Whoever sleeps in it has to go downstairs after midnight and raid the fridge." She took out a list and passed it around. There were ten items on the list. Ice Cream, apples, chocolate, grapes… The girls all looked carefully at this list.

"Popcorn and biscuits are not kept in the fridge." Alyssa stared at Jess so as to show her how stupid she thought Jasmine was.

"No, but you will have to search for these. They are somewhere in the kitchen."

Jess pointed to the list in shock. "Wine!" she gasped.

"My dad has three small bottles downstairs. Two are in the fridge and one is in the lounge!" Jasmine giggled.

Jess looked petrified. Her eyes seemed to get bigger as she stared at the other girls and her mouth formed a letter 'o' shape.

"You look like a constipated chimpanzee," Alyssa muttered and this set Jasmine off into a fit of giggles.

Jasmine suddenly stopped "Ooh, I've wet myself," she screamed rushing out to the bathroom.

This was the first time that day Alyssa and Jess had been alone. There was an awkward silence between them. After a while, Alyssa looked at Jess. "Are you OK, Jess?"

Jess shrugged her shoulders to show she was not sure. "I think I will be alright on the floor after all. I could never go creeping about downstairs in somebody else's house. Too much of a coward, really. My dad is always telling me I should stick up for myself more often. He expects so much from me and I often feel guilty about letting him down." She came over and sat next to Alyssa. "I thought Jasmine was really horrible to you today! I am sorry, I did not help you when she threw the mud at you."

Alyssa shrugged her shoulders. "Don't worry about it! Come over here and give me a hug and thank you for telling me this."

When Jasmine came back into the room and saw both girls in an embrace, she scowled.

"Ooh, is it kissy kissy time?" She scowled and started pacing around the bedroom muttering in a sing-song voice, "Lissy Lissy kissy kissy."

Alyssa sighed. She knew she would have to do the midnight challenge. She would not let Jasmine gain an advantage by refusing to do it. There would be rumours spread around the school next term about her being a coward as well as Jess!

The girls chatted until midnight. The conversations were about boys who they thought were hot. Jasmine couldn't resist implying that Alyssa had grabbed Toby from behind her back. But Alyssa ignored the comments and the matter was dropped. They made a list of boys to chase next term, most of them a couple of years ahead of them. Older guys seemed to be the fashion at the moment.

"Peter Matlock has such beautiful eyes." Sighed Jess.

"Shame about him picking his nose all the time. I would be frightened, I might end up eating his bogies if I kissed him," replied Jasmine.

Jess was interested to know more about the amount of freedom Alyssa was given at home. "It seems you are always allowed to go where you want. Not like me! I am virtually a prisoner at home," she grumbled.

"That's because her parents don't love her enough," whispered Jasmine, nodding her head and staring at Alyssa.

"That's a horrible thing to say!" Alyssa snapped. She was getting really fed up with Jasmine's attitude and her desire to make everybody feel unhappy. "I am allowed out by myself as my parents trust me to behave and not get into trouble."

"Aren't you afraid of getting attacked late at night?" asked Jess.

Alyssa shrugged. "Not really! Anyway, my Taekwondo training is a useful thing to have and I would use it if necessary, now I have a green belt."

"Such a brave girl!" Jasmine was sitting on her bed and jumped up looking at her watch. "It's midnight, so let's see how brave this girl is in facing my challenge!"

Alyssa sighed getting up from the floor and asked Jasmine for the list.

"Oh you don't get a second chance to look at those items, I would have thought you would have been able to remember them!"

Alyssa gritted her teeth and attempted a smile. She quietly opened the door and started creeping down the stairs. Jasmine dashed to the door and peered around making sure Alyssa had gone. She turned and with a wicked smile on her face, tearing the list up as she sat on the bed next to Jess. She looked at Jess. "What list?" She winked. "Now make sure if questioned later, you had no idea about a list being made tonight."

Jess frowned. "What do you mean?"

"So this is the first part of, 'Trap Alyssa'. We will make sure my parents find her downstairs looking through draws and cupboards. She will be a thief in the making!" She turned to Ruffie who was asleep on the rug. "Ruffie is a well-trained guard dog. My father is a police dog handler. He trained him to react badly to any intruder or potential thief. All you need to say is 'Ruffie Seek Thief' and he will be off to bite anyone he finds in the house who is not one of the family." Ruffie, who was snoozing on the bed, sat bolt upright growling and ready to pounce. "Down Ruffie," whispered Jasmine. She turned to stare at Jess. "See what I mean?"

Jess looked both worried and confused. "But why are you doing this?" she stammered. "What has Alyssa done to you?" She paused and gasped as she realised what was really going on between the two girls. "It's Toby, isn't it? You are still jealous of him seeing Alyssa and her being caught stealing in your house will make them split up!"

Jasmine laughed. "You clever old thing. When Toby finds out about this and then sees her covered in dog bites, he will not be so eager to go out with her anymore and his parents will make sure he doesn't see her again. So then I will be there to help him get over the break-up. Their divorce! So to speak." She giggled. "And won't he feel sorry for me? Going around with a thief. I will definitely need a shoulder to cry on."

"Jasmine that's awful, poor Alyssa," Jess cried.

"Is it?" Jasmine hissed. She spun around as she thought of another idea. "Another thing." She paused. "You will be helping me!"

"No, I shan't. I think you are being manipulative and cruel when Toby finds out what you have done, he will not want to see you anyway!"

Jasmine stopped pacing and grabbed Jess by her hair forcing her head back so that she was staring into her face. "So how would you like me to tell your parents, especially your father how much of a liar you are? Pretending to have asthma so as to get a comfy bed. He would see you for the 'wimp' you really are!"

Jess became very flustered as Jasmine let go of her hair. It was true her father always told her to 'lead from the front'. Be strong. Stand up for herself. Being honest and true. She had made a start by sharing this with Alyssa earlier that night. Her father would love her to take outward bound courses, go hiking in the mountains. All of this scared her to bits. "Wait a minute, you really must not tell my parents about this!" She began to snivel and whimper. "They will kill me! Please Jasmine, do not tell."

"Well then all you need to do is when I give you the signal you will say 'Ruffie Seek Thief'."

Jess looked sick; panic was etched onto her face as she stared at the wall refusing to look at the girl and her dog that was still sleeping like a baby on the rug. After a few minutes, she sighed, turned and nodded her head. Jasmine raised her hand and pointed to the dog. Jess got up and stood next to Ruffie. "Ruffie Seek Thief," she said in a very weak voice.

"Louder, idiot!" spat Jasmine, screwing up her face that mirrored the hate she felt for the girl who was at that moment creeping down the stairs.

"Ruffie Seek Thief!" shouted Jess who then burst into tears.

Alyssa was at the bottom of the stairs. The house was in darkness everyone had gone to bed. She was not happy about doing this. But if it meant improving things between her and Jasmine it might just be worth it. She remembered the lounge was off to her right and once her eyes became accustomed to the darkness she could see shapes, they were armchairs and the sofa. Looming up like small hills on an alien landscape. She nearly tripped over a small table and instinctively her hand went out to catch a vase. She remembered looking at this before when dancing in the lounge earlier. It was light blue in colour and had serpents crawling around the base. It looked expensive. Alyssa stood still for a moment so as to calm her rapid heartbeats. She crept towards the large cabinet with the glass doors on the back wall. Should she turn on the light? It might risk waking Jasmine's parents. *Too risky,* she thought. But she had noticed there was a light inside the cabinet. She could use this as it would not be as bright as the other lights in the lounge. She opened the glass door and felt around for the switch. Yes, she was in luck. Gently, she switched it on and this just gave enough light to see what was inside. It was a drinks cupboard and amongst the bottle of gin and whisky, there were two miniature bottles of red wine. She looked at the label, it said 'Cotes Du Rhone 53cls' on the label. She stuffed each of these in her pyjama pockets. Jasmine said there were three bottles so the other one must be in the fridge. She was beginning to feel more confident now that she had found some of the items on the list. She turned around trying to find her way to the kitchen and suddenly froze. A dark shape was standing at the bottom of the stairs. A throaty growl seemed to be coming from it. She began to sweat and at the same time shiver giving her goosebumps across her arms and legs. She suddenly felt very weak. "Ruffie?" she whispered, crouching down as she hoped the dog would recognise her as a friendly guest. But this only made the dog growl louder ending with a snarl. "Ruffie good dog, good dog, come here boy." The animal pounced and Alyssa dived to her left rolling over on the carpet. The two wine bottles in her pocket fell out and rolled across the floor leaving a couple of bruises on each hip. She felt like screaming out in pain but managed to keep quiet so as not to wake everybody up. She needn't have bothered. The dog smashed into the small table which overturned sending the pretty little vase flying through the air and smashing to pieces on the floor. Ruffie was slipping and sliding on the wooden floor. His paws used as paddles as he desperately tried for another pounce. This gave Alyssa just enough time to run out of the lounge and into the kitchen. Followed closely by a snarling beast from hell, not like the docile happy dog that wanted its tummy tickled earlier on. Alyssa stumbled through the kitchen knocking over two kitchen stools. The noise was deafening as one of the stools had ricocheted off the washing machine spinning like a top before crashing to the floor. Alyssa had her back against the kitchen door and felt a stabbing pain in her bottom. She groaned putting her hand behind her and grasped the door key. She thought this must be like being caned in Victorian times. A recent history lesson coming back to haunt her. It was such a stupid thought, she began to laugh. But suddenly stopped as the dog now hearing the noise would be able to find her. Ruffie raced towards her. Another dark shape shot in front of Alyssa and seemed to attach itself to the dog's face. By accident Alyssa's arm slammed into the light switch. She could not believe what she saw. A cat and a dog involved in a screaming circle of pain and clatter rolling about on the floor. Quickly, she unlocked the door and ran out into the garden.

As she was running across the lawn she heard shouts coming from the house as Jasmine's parents rushed down the stairs. She did not wait to see them. Leaping over the garden fence she kept running out onto the street. She did not stop until she arrived home. She realised she had run home in her pyjamas.

Chinilan (Fed Up Weary)

Liam woke up, still thinking about those questions of yesterday. Why did the old lady and the children seem so afraid of Snickitylickers? Why was the cat protecting him from Jal? It was as though the cat had selected him for a purpose. Maybe to help in some way? The badge of honour. What was that all about? It sounded like a very old-fashioned statement. It had a military flavour. He would have to ask Jal more about this the next time they met.

He looked at his alarm clock. It had a picture of a spider man on the dial with his arm being the second hand with a finger that pointed to the seconds as it ticked around. It was 6.10. He thought he would go down to the kitchen to get an early breakfast. Chocolate Weetabix, dry with no milk and a cup of tea would do. He looked up and there sat Snickitylickers, outside on the kitchen windowsill. Liam noticed that intense stare from those green eyes. There were scratch marks and bald patches where some cat fur had been torn out on her side. He went and opened the window and the cat jumped in and went straight through the kitchen and hall to the front door. She sat staring at him. As soon as Liam got to the door, the cat ran up the stairs. The last thing he wanted was the cat to jump on his parents' bed and wake them up.

But Snickitylickers went into his sister's room. Liam poked his head around the door and saw the cat sitting on Alyssa's pillow. Alyssa was fast asleep. He thought she was having a 'sleep in' at Jasmine's house? He went to grab the cat who hissed at him jumping back, getting her claws caught up in Alyssa's hair. She screamed at this shock awakening. "What the hell is happening?" she cried. Seeing Liam standing over her bed. "Liam, how dare you sneak into my room!" She saw the cat with strands of her hair stuck in its claws. Her mood suddenly changed. Snickitylickers' intense stares seemed to calm her down. "Hello, my beauty, where did you come from?" She glared at her brother. "You didn't steal her from somewhere, Liam, did you?"

"What!" shouted Liam. "I did not! She was sitting on the kitchen window sill and I let her in."

"Keep your voice down, idiot, you will wake up the whole house." Alyssa jumped out of bed, clutching her side; she had purple bruises on each of her thighs caused when she fell over in Jasmine's lounge, rolling over the wine bottles in her pocket and a small cut in her bottom when she accidentally stabbed herself on the key in the kitchen door. She groaned and limped towards her wardrobe. The cat followed her and sat at the entrance to her room staring at the girl.

"What happened to you last night?"

"I will tell you later!" Alyssa looked at the cat. "She seems to want us to follow her."

"When I let her in, she went straight to the front door. I followed her and then she rushed up to your room. It is as though she knew you were here but she has never been to this house before?" Liam scratched his head. "This is really weird." He then told his sister where he went with the cat

42

yesterday to the gypsy camp and his fight with Jal. "This cat saved me from being cut by Jal with his flick knife up in the treehouse. She really wanted me to visit them. It seems they are all frightened of the cat."

Alyssa told Liam of her experiences at the party and the fight with the dog and the mystery attacker who enabled her to escape. "I think this is the cat that saved me from the dog. I dread to think of what Mum will say when she hears from Jasmine's parents." She frowned. "I need to keep away from home for a bit!"

Both children turned to look at the cat. She let out a loud meow, stretched lazily and trotted down the stairs and sat by the front door.

"Well, I think she wants us to follow her." Liam looked pensively at his sister. "What do you think?"

"Hmm." Alyssa looked thoughtful. "Actually, it's just what I need. It will stop me from thinking about my explanations as to why I left Jasmine at 1 o'clock in the morning. It will also keep me out of Mum and Dad's way today." Alyssa smiled. "I think we should get dressed and follow the cat."

Liam rushed into his room to get changed. He was quite pleased that today he would have his sister with him.

Alyssa quickly scribbled a note for their parents saying they had gone out. 'Came home early, had a fight with Jasmine.' She decided to tell the truth as she knew Jasmine's parents would be contacting her parents first thing in the morning. She grabbed a doughnut from the fridge. Snickitylickers had run out of the house and was waiting for them on the corner of the street. She kept stopping to check that the children were following and jumped over the gate to the Gypsy site, running between the caravans until she disappeared.

Both children stopped at the gate. Everything seemed very quiet. Liam noticed the door to Jal's caravan was open and swinging backwards and forwards in the breeze. "That's the caravan where Jal and Rawnie live!" He peered inside. "It's empty." The place seemed abandoned.

"Look, there's the cat," shouted Liam, running over to the fence at the back of the campsite. The cat squeezed itself underneath a gap in the fence pushing her through overgrown bracken and thick foliage. Liam went to follow.

"Liam, be careful. Where are you going?" Alyssa was worried. It was her first visit to the campsite and she imagined angry gipsies suddenly appearing and chasing them away.

"The cat wants us to follow her. Stay there if you want to!" Liam started climbing over the fence. It was a high rickety wooden fence and as he clambered to the top, he thought he heard it sigh as it collapsed under his weight tumbling him into a bunch of brambles and nettles. He was covered in scratches and had two angry red patches on his arms and legs but he did not seem to notice due to his desire to follow the cat at all costs. But where was the adventure playground, the moat and the treehouse. They seemed to have vanished. Just the two empty caravans in a field.

Alyssa walked over the broken fence, it was too late to start worrying about the damage Liam had caused and she resigned to following her brother, so broke into a run as she saw Liam disappear over the top of the hill. As soon as she arrived at the top of the hill, she saw Liam standing in front of an old timber framed cottage, it had a sloping thatched roof. She walked up to Liam who turned around and said the cat had gone around the back of the house and then vanished.

"I am going inside, she must have gone through a window."

"Look." Alyssa pointed to the single window at the front of the house. "These houses did not have more than one window so you would have seen her if she did get in."

Liam was determined to enter and walked up to the door to try to open it. It would not open! He started kicking the door and pushing on the wooden bar that was fixed firmly across the door slotted into two wooden joints at each end.

"Stop that, Liam!" shouted his sister. "Just let's think carefully before you break the door." If this was a genuine medieval cottage it would be a shame to damage it. It certainly did not look like one of the cottages that had been built on the medieval site they had visited on a school trip last term. If they could ease the large wooden bar out of the joints at either side of the door it might open.

Liam started aimlessly kicking the grass and walking around in circles. "Humph! I just want to get inside, I'm sure the cat is in there."

"No, she's not. Look on the roof!"

Liam glanced up to see Snickitylickers sitting on the top of the roof licking herself. On seeing the children, she walked over to the edge and jumped, running down the wall and off to a little bunch of bluebells. The children followed.

"What's this?" Alyssa crouched down as she saw something shiny underneath one of the bluebells. It was an old rusty key.

Liam grabbed it. "This must be the key to the door!" The children ran back to the cottage. Liam stared at the door. "Where's the keyhole! This is really weird, man!"

Alyssa glanced down at the bottom of the door and just to the side was a metal box. She picked it up and grabbed the key from Liam. It did not fit but the lid sprang open. Inside what looked like an old piece of parchment wrapped in leaves that were tied by a length of twine. Carefully, she unwrapped the little parcel and spread the parchment out on the grass. At the top of the page was the name:

Liam looked puzzled and glanced at his sister.

"I think it says Master Ott," said Alyssa. She rolled the parchment out again and there was a drawing of a man, he was naked.

Liam burst out laughing. "How gross!"

Underneath the picture was the word,

Then there were three more pictures of wrestlers.

Both children just stared at each other. "What does this all mean?" whispered Alyssa.

Hamishagos
(To Meddle or Disturb)

Alyssa sat in the lounge at home with her 'iPad' on her lap. Liam was sitting beside her looking bored. "Come on let's go back to see that cottage and try and open that door!"

Alyssa sighed thinking why boys were so impatient. He was likely just to go back by himself. He was squirming about on the sofa as though he had an itchy bum. "Liam, you know that I am not allowed out because of what happened at Jasmine's house the other day. Mum and Dad are hardly speaking to me. They also blame me for taking you with me when we visited the gypsy encampment. And..." She turned around to glare at him. "I noticed you never said anything in my defence. It was your idea we go and follow that cat in the first place."

Liam slumped back on the sofa digging his chin into his chest and staring at the carpet. He was feeling a bit ashamed of himself but would certainly not admit this to his sister.

Alyssa had typed in 'medieval wrestling' on the 'iPad' and had copied down a list of books on the subject. "Wow, they are so expensive," she cried. "The cheapest one is £22. Wait a minute, let's see if the library has anything." She continued typing to find their local library website. She was in luck. "Modern Practice of a fifteenth-century Art by Jessica Finley." She read out. "Liam get into town to pick this up!" As she clicked on the correct file. "This will be held for 24 hours."

Liam jumped up and was just about to dash out the front door.

"Wait!" shouted Alyssa. "You will need the reserve slip, so just wait until I have printed it out. Do you have anything inside that head of yours?"

After waiting an hour, which seemed like five hours to Alyssa, she had managed to find the meaning of the word 'derutat'; it was a Romani word for 'puzzled'.

Liam returned with the book. "I will read it first." Liam smiled, holding the book away from Alyssa so she could not get hold of it.

"Pig!" shouted his sister and as she was taller than Liam snatched the book away from him. "Now sit down and listen! You know I am a quicker reader than you are. Anyway, you can sit beside me and we can read this together."

Liam took one look at the amount of print on each page. "Doesn't have many pictures, does it? Boring!"

Alyssa started reading and after a few minutes, Liam started listening. Master Ott was Jewish and was a wrestler to the Austrian princes. He wrote instructions for practising the different wrestling moves. It was often used as a defence tactic when a swordsman lost his sword in battle and then started using his hands and arms to pull and push the opponent. So the main aim was to get your opponent onto their back for two seconds. She suddenly stopped and stood up, the book dropping to the floor. There was a picture showing an opponent who had lost his sword grabbing and pulling his opponent just as he had started lunging at him with the sword. "So by pulling somebody who is already trying to stab or push you it would mean them falling forward onto the ground. That was the first picture we saw wrapped around the key."

She paused and walked to the window lost in thought. "Liam, there were other pictures, where are they?"

"Oh, I stuffed them in my pocket and I think Mum took them to wash later." Liam rushed upstairs to his bedroom and returned holding the dirty pair of shorts. He turned the pockets inside out and the packet taken from the cottage fell onto the floor. There were three pictures.

The first showed one wrestler pulling his opponent over. The second showed the opposite; an opponent being pushed over backwards.

The third picture showed two wrestlers hugging each other pulling themselves closer together. "Still doesn't make any sense to me," moaned Liam. "We still could not open that door with the key."

"But say the key was not meant to open the front door, maybe it is a key for a door inside the house." Alyssa smiled. "I think the pictures are the clue to opening that door so we can enter the cottage with the key!"

"We need to go back to the cottage now, sis."

Alyssa knew that Liam would have been gone in a moment, reluctantly agreed. *God knows what Mum and Dad will think about me breaking curfew,* she thought.

The children stood together outside the cottage and Alyssa took out the three pictures and laid them out on the grass. Liam, meanwhile, had started pulling and tugging at the door, rattling the handle. Alyssa could tell he was still as frustrated as ever at not being able to get in.

"Liam, calm down, come over here and help me with the pictures."

Liam turned around and glared at Alyssa but then saw the determined look on her face so he knew he would not get any more help if he did not do as he was told. He slouched over to his sister plonking himself down on the grass.

"Liam, can you remember which picture was the first to be wrapped around the key?"

"That one!" He pointed to the picture with one of the wrestlers pulling the other over. Alyssa put the picture above the other two. Liam then pointed to what he thought was the second picture that had been wrapped around the first. It showed one wrestler pushing the other over on his back.

"So this must be the third one then." Alyssa picked up the last picture with two wrestlers cramped down low on the ground each gabbing each other's bottoms trying to pull each other over. Alyssa got up and stared at the three pictures.

"Well, come on genius, how does this help open this door?"

"OK, this is just a guess but I think that the actions shown by the pictures we need to use on the door. So the first picture shows wrestlers pushing each other and the other two show them pulling and then pushing each other. If we, therefore, grasp the door and push it, and then pull and push it, do you think it will open?" Alyssa looked quite pleased with this piece of deduction.

Liam went over to the door and grasped the large wooden bar that was placed across the front of the door. He quickly pulled then pushed and pulled the bar in and out. Nothing happened.

"Try doing it slowly." Again nothing happened. "Let me try." Alyssa grasped the bar but again nothing happened.

The children kept trying different methods of the pulling and pushing sequences. Trying very quickly then very slowly. Then pausing between each action. Still, the door stayed stubbornly shut. They could not even move the bar a tiny bit. They tried holding the bar together. Nothing seemed to work.

Liam was getting impatient. "Let's smash the door down." He went hunting for a large stone while Alyssa studied the pictures again. The first picture also had swords scattered on the ground with one wrestler standing over two swords lying across each other in a 'cross' pattern. Suddenly, Liam returned with a huge boulder and was marching up to the door with it raised above his head ready to throw it at the door.

"Stop, you idiot," screamed his sister. "If you damage the door, I am going home and will not help you anymore."

Liam stopped undecided, still holding the boulder over his head. His arms started aching under the strain. He then threw the boulder away and stomped off into the woods.

"Liam, come back." She ran into the woods and grabbed Liam's arm pulling him back towards the cottage. As she was dragging her brother through the undergrowth, Snickitylickers ran out behind an old oak tree. The children stopped and watched as she went and sat next to the door. Alyssa went to pick her up but the cat then ran off and disappeared behind a mound of earth. Both children ran after

51

her. There was a rusty old BBQ turned on its side amongst other rubbish. Liam started kicking through the litter. Broken bottles, beer cans, rusty skewers used for putting meat on spits for the BBQ. The cat suddenly pounced on these as though they were prey.

Liam laughed. "Look, Snickitylickers wants to play." He picked up one of the skewers and dangled it enticingly above the cat's head. Snickitylickers jumped up with her front paws stretched out in an attempt to grab the metal rods. Then started chasing Liam as he ran, putting the skewers in his back pocket. "On guard!" he shouted, holding the skewers one in each hand. "Lord Liam superhero extraordinaire and his trusty swords will conquer all who comes across his path!"

Alyssa sighed. "Come on superhero, use some of those powers of yours to open the door," in an attempt to bring his mind back to the present.

Liam wandered back. The cat followed him and started studying the pictures again. The cat went and sat on the first picture. "Hey silly!" He pushed Snickitylickers off the picture. But the cat went back and sat on it again. Liam started laughing. "What are you doing, stupid cat?"

"Maybe she is not as stupid as you think. She might just be trying to tell us something!" mused his sister. "Let's have a closer look at that first picture again. What have we missed?" Both children looked carefully at the picture again.

"The crossed swords!" Liam said.

"Yes and the way that wrestler is standing with each foot on either side of the cross pattern," replied Alyssa. She paused in thought. "Those skewers you found in the rubbish and the way the cat reacted when you picked them up. She also led us over to the rubbish. It is as if she wanted us to find them."

Liam nodded. "Yes, and I was using them as swords when playing with the cat!" Liam was becoming excited.

"So if we put the two skewers down in front of the door in the shape of a cross and one of us stands over them as in that first picture. Do you think that may open the door?"

Liam sniggered. "Don't see how that can be correct, but we could try!"

Alyssa jumped up and went to the door. "Now put the skewers down like they were the swords in the picture." Liam carefully laid them down glancing back at the picture to make sure they were in the correct position. "Now put each of your feet in the same position as the wrestler." Alyssa then put her hands on Liam's shoulders taking the part of the second wrestler. "Liam now pull on that bar while I pull on your shoulders! We will pull together on the count of three. One... two... three."

Nothing happened!

Liam spun around in anger. "So much for your stupid ideas!" he shouted.

"Look, be patient. There are three pictures, remember. Maybe they show a sequence of actions." Alyssa bent down and poured over the second picture but became irritated at Liam pacing around like a spring antelope. She walked away holding the second picture to a quieter place to think. "Hmm..." whispering to herself. "Now, this picture shows the wrestler pushing his opponent, but also twisting his shoulder in an anti-clockwise movement down to the ground. Right, Liam, come here, I want you to practice the movements in the second picture with me."

Liam came over to the door and both children discussed what they were going to do. Liam grabbed hold of the bar with

53

his left hand and placed his other hand on Alyssa's right shoulder as they both pushed together, Liam twisted the bar in an anti-clockwise direction and in a downward movement.

"Before you start another 'hissy fit', remember this is the second sequence and nothing will happen, I think until we put all three movements together," Alyssa snapped.

The third picture showed a pulling action. Both children went into a hug with their hands on each other's backsides. They practised each sequence many times until they felt happy with the result.

"OK!" Alyssa wiped the sweat off her forehead. "Now, let's try again."

They managed the first two sequences very well and this time the bar was beginning to move with every turn which was an encouraging sign. When it came to the third sequence, Alyssa pulled Liam hard. The back pocket of his jeans must have become entangled with the bar. The door seemed to shake and the hinges screeched as the wooden bar seemed to shoot up into the air. Slowly, it swung open leaving the children in an untidy heap but on the inside of the house. "Yes," Liam shouted, jumping up and raising his fist in the air, "high-five, Sis," as both children smacked their hands together.

The children were standing in a long corridor with rooms on each side. "This is nothing like the inside of a medieval cottage, they only had a couple of rooms; one in which they kept animals and another for cooking and sleeping in." Alyssa frowned. Everything smelt damp and dark. There was an earth floor and with every step they took, small clouds of dust rose from underneath their feet. The walls were smothered with ivy. Buddleia and brambles were festooned across the floor.

Wild mushrooms which had grown up to ankle height. Alyssa wondered how this was possible as there was not much natural light for them to reproduce.

"Weird, really weird man!" Liam was wandering up and down the corridor pushing open the doors and quickly looking inside. "It's a bit like Dr Who's Tardis," he said. "Much bigger on the inside than on the outside." But the first room was empty, just an earth floor giving them a musty smell. Liam turned around to see Snickitylickers prowling in through the main door. "Hi beautiful, now that you have managed to get us into this place, what do we do now?"

The cat, now purring, sat in front of Liam staring up at him. Suddenly, it sprang up grabbing his shorts and climbing up to sit on top of his shoulders. "Ouch." Liam jumped backwards rubbing his legs where the cat had scratched him. "You little beast!" he cried and then burst out laughing. Snickitylickers did not stay on his shoulders long and jumped back down and went through the door to the first room. The door banged shut again with a screech as the rusty hinges complained of the sudden movement.

Alyssa went to push the door open but it was firmly shut. A piece of what looked like old parchment floated out from underneath the door. She picked it up. The writing was in a similar style to the printed sheets showing the wrestling movements. The heading was the same. DERUTAT. "That means a puzzle," she said.

"God, not another one," groaned Liam. "What does it say?"

Alyssa continued to read.

'My sister is green with envy but do not eat her as you will get poisoned. She likes climbing walls.'

Liam stuck out his chin and began to pout. "I hate puzzles! It's not fair when you think you are getting somewhere, there seems to be another challenge or problem to solve."

Alyssa remained thoughtful and stared around the short corridor. Liam grabbed part of an ivy plant tearing it off the wall and flinging it down on the floor. There were only two rooms in the cottage, one on each side of the corridor. A hawthorn branch was propped against the door to the room on the left while the door on the right looked easier to open.

"That's it!" shouted Alyssa. "Ivy. It's green and climbs up walls and Ivy is the name of a girl!" There was another screech of the rusty hinges as the door to the room on the right swung slowly open.

The children ran into the room expecting to see the cat and nothing else. They had checked the rooms before and they were all empty. But not this room. There was no sign of the cat. A swirling green mist seemed to surround them and all they could see were shapes outlined in the haze. Alyssa grabbed Liam's hand as she was frightened of losing him. Normally, Liam would have been embarrassed, snatching his hand away. But feeling lost he was grateful for having his sister close to him. He stretched out his hands, swinging them from side to side in front of him so as to stop him colliding with any of the strange shapes. A low moaning sound grew louder, making the hair on the back of his neck tingle. Flashes of lightening exploded into the room and for a brief moment Alyssa saw the numbers '1841 'scrawled across the wall. She started to shake, feeling weak she gripped Liam's hand even tighter. The swirling mist seemed to get thicker and glow with colours changing from red through to green. It was as if there was a giant rainbow inside the room. The moaning sound turned into a high-pitched whistle. Both children put their hands over their ears and crouched down on the earth floor. Their eyes started stinging and streaming with moisture. The earth floor seemed to change its shape, with small hillocks of earth rising up in front of them and suddenly sinking into a 'sink hole' ready to swallow them. Liam, now shaking, stared into the black abyss in front of him. He could not move. Paralysed with fear. He felt he was being pulled into a hollow slimy tunnel. He was so tired, his face wet from his tears. All he wanted to do was to sleep.

Alyssa coughing and choking, her eyes streaming and tears pouring down her face. She saw Liam's body go stiff and his head drop forward. "Liam focus. Keep awake." She screamed, reaching out to grasp his shoulder so as to stop him from falling forward. Sparks seemed to fly from his shoulders as she touched him, burning her hands and forcing her body to summersault backwards. She collided with something solid and vaguely heard a loud crack as her head hit something sharp. Her head felt warm and something sticky started sliding down her cheek. This was the last thing that she remembered before she lost consciousness. Her shouting at Liam did keep him awake. He started fighting the tiredness that seemed to trickle into his arms and legs. He began to tense his body starting with his hands and slowly pushing himself, arching his back and kicking with his feet. Very slowly, he began to pull himself across the floor until he reached his sister. He turned around and grabbed her in what looked like a bear hug. Shutting his eyes and burying his face in her hair. It felt like he was in a tent being shaken by a terrible storm.

"Alyssa," he croaked. An eerie silence. "Alyssa," he shouted, "are you OK?" Again, there was no response but

Liam noticed the mist was beginning to clear and the room seemed to settle down. Everything became quiet. Liam pulled himself up into a sitting position. Looking around, he began to recognise the furniture. Two parakeets in a cage and a tropical fish tank. "Stranger, stranger!" the parakeets chorused, sticking their heads out and strutting around the cage. He seemed to be back in Jal's grandmother's caravan. *That is impossible,* he thought. Looking down at the floor he noticed he was lying on a carpet and not on the earth floor. He looked down at Alyssa lying flat on her back. Eyes closed with blood streaming down the side of her face. "Oh God, Alyssa." She was looking very 'corpse like'. Liam stumbled to his feet and went to the sink. He grabbed a tea towel from the rail. Returning to his sister and gently mopping her face. He was not sure what to do next. He vaguely remembered you should roll over an injured person onto their side so began to turn his sister over and to his relief, she started coughing and moaning. "Alyssa, so glad to see you, sis!" Blinking back the tears. He realised that her shouting at him had saved him from something evil that he did not want to think about.

"Oh, my head hurts!" Alyssa sat up rubbing the side of her face. "Where are we? What happened?"

"We are in the grandmother's caravan on the gypsy site. This is where I met 'Granny Pat' when visiting the site yesterday with Rawnie and Jal."

"It's beautiful." Alyssa looking around and getting up to have a closer look at the parakeets, she stuck her finger through the bars of their cage. "Aren't they sweet?" She smiled, forgetting her headache on seeing the two birds.

"Stranger, stranger," the birds replied sticking their heads to the side and staring at the girl.

Alyssa laughed. "Yes, I suppose we are strangers to you." Suddenly, the creatures in the fish tank started swimming very fast and the children looked in amazement as their speed sent small waves through the tank that started to shake. The parakeets on seeing this started hopping up and down on their perches. "Stanger, stranger." They squawked. "Mullo, Mullo, Mullo!"

Liam glanced at the fish tank. The little creatures seemed to be swimming in a frenzy making the surface water look quite choppy. Parts of the underwater plants had been pushed onto the glass. Liam took a closer look. Squashed plant remains seemed to spell out the word 'HEDGE'.

Liam's heart was beating so fast and Alyssa's face lit up in a cheeky smile. "Wow," she cried. "We have another puzzle to solve!"

On hearing this, Liam groaned, placed his hands over his head. "Not another puzzle!"

Leaving the cottage and walking back across the encampment, Liam noticed Granny Pat's caravan was missing. In fact, there were only a couple of small near-derelict caravans scattered across the field. Alyssa had not seen what the site looked like before they entered the cottage. When Liam was describing the scene, she wondered if he had been dreaming knowing how easy it was for him to drift off into a world of his own.

"Liam, are you sure you did see these people on the site yesterday? Dad did tell me the travellers had been evicted from the site last week and had moved on!"

"Look, I know what I saw and who I met! We have just been inside 'Granny Pat's' caravan and now it has vanished!"

Liam growled. "Don't care what you think!" He started walking quickly so as to get away from his sister.

Alyssa sighed and slowed down so as to give her brother a bit of space. She knew if she continued to challenge him over this it would only make matters worse. Liam seemed to be ahead of his time. A teenager bottled into an eight-year-old body!

Mush (Friend)

The next couple of days, the children stayed at home. Alyssa had received a telling off from both of her parents together. They were both very angry. In fact, she had never seen her father in such a state. Her mother had to go around to Jasmine's house to apologise and to try and stop her parents from informing the police. They had paid for the damage caused. The broken vase. Damage to the kitchen door and they had to replace a couple of kitchen chairs. The bill coming to £350. Her father had stopped her allowance of £10 per month. This would be cancelled until the debt had been settled. She quickly calculated that she would be 16 before she received another penny! Jasmine's parents did not want to see Alyssa anywhere near their daughter in future. Jess's parents had also phoned and told her parents to keep her away from their daughter. Things looked very bleak and she probably lost Toby's friendship but was too scared to phone him up to see how he felt. She just had to 'lie low' and keep out of the way of trouble, having the puzzles to solve in connection with the travellers would be something to take her mind off being the most unpopular girl in the neighbourhood.

Alyssa sat on her bed staring out of her window, her shoulders drooped she just wanted a bit of space to be on her own to think things over. There was a knock on her bedroom door and Jenny Durtnall walked in and came and sat on the bed next to her daughter. She gave Alyssa a hug. "Alyssa, I know you have had a lot of challenges recently! I just wanted to say both your dad and I love you and we are proud of the way you always look out for Liam and keep him out of trouble."

Alyssa turned around burying her face in her mother's chest. Tears began to flow as she realised this is what she really wanted to hear. "I am sorry for causing you and Dad these problems and I promise I will find a job soon to help pay you and Dad back!"

This brought tears to Jenny's eyes as she thought if only I had more time to spend with my daughter I might have been able to have seen the trouble she was getting into with Jasmine and her parents. After speaking to Jasmine recently, she could see that Jasmine was both jealous of Alyssa and could be such a manipulative little girl. "Now, Alyssa in future you must confide in me more often when things happen with your friends as two minds are better than one."

Alyssa smiled. "Thanks, Mum!"

Liam also did not get away with it. Although most of the blame was seen to be his sisters. Alyssa being the eldest. He was also 'grounded'. Forbidden to have friends around for a week. However, he had owned up to persuading his sister to come with him to the gypsy encampment and to be the one who started breaking into the cottage. He had asked his father about whether the gipsies had been moved on and was told they left over two weeks ago. The local police had moved them on. So he could not understand his experiences at the campsite a couple of days ago. Both children were confined to the house. Alyssa had persuaded Liam to help her in trying to make any sense of what had happened.

Both children were in Alyssa's bedroom sitting on her bed with Alyssa holding her 'Swedish Fairy' doll her uncle had given her as a baby. In times of trouble, she would carry this around with her as it made her feel loved. Even though she was now 13. She put the doll down and grabbed a pen and started scribbling in her notebook.

"Let's make a list so that we have a chance of getting to the bottom of this."

"As you do all the writing." Liam smiled. "I will draw the pictures." He laughed.

"Idiot, why would we need pictures?"

"Hmmm! Don't think this is stupid. After all, I am the only one to have seen Granny Pat, Jal and Rawnie I can sketch them. This might come in useful later!"

"OK, you have a point there, go and get your sketch pad and make a start." Alyssa knew Liam liked sketching and he was quite good at it.

The children worked well together. Both became interested in trying to make some sense of what had happened over the last couple of days. After an hour, Alyssa put her pen down and looked at the list. She had written the heading followed by a number of questions and her ideas of how these could be answered.

MYSTERY   GYPSY   ENCAMPMENT.   WHAT   IS HAPPENING HERE?

1 How can Liam's experience of meeting the cat, the gipsies at the encampment last week be explained when they had left the site two weeks ago?

2 What did the old lady mean when she told Liam to seek justice and honour for the sake of their destiny?

3 What happened at the cottage? Sequence of pictures from medieval times to open the door, was it magic?

4 What do the strange words mean?

5 Why are the travellers afraid of the cat?

Alyssa yawned. "Well, I think that is enough for us to be getting on with. Have you finished the sketches of the gipsies?"

Liam nodded and handed her the three pictures. Granny Pat resembled an 'old hag' or witch with a grainy face with hairs sprouting out of her chin, her head wrapped in a scarf. She had one tooth missing at the front giving her an eerie appearance. Jal, he had drawn, looking like a tanned Italian. A sharp, jutting chin, dark hair and green eyes. Quite muscular in appearance as though he was used to doing a lot of physical work like digging and lifting heavy objects. Rawnie looked very much like her brother with the same tanned appearance and black hair that looked a bit messy. For a girl, she was also quite muscular and with a stocky build.

"OK, Liam, I think we are ready to start." Both children gave each other a 'high-five'.

Action

The next couple of days, the children were kept busy in trying to answer the questions on Alyssa's list. It was agreed that Liam would be on his very best behaviour and would take on some housekeeping tasks. Like tidying his room and doing the vacuuming. Both their parents were busy and would be delighted to see the change in him. Then he would ask to go out to see friends. However, the real reason would be to deliver his flyers about a missing cat and posting these around the neighbourhood, so as to get more details as to who owned Snickitylickers. It might help explain why the cat was always around their area as nobody in their street owned her. Meanwhile, Alyssa would look into the history of Martin Shaw Wood. This was easy as her father was a volunteer and worked for the forestry commission and often joined a team to cut back vegetation to give the 36 species of trees space to grow within the 254 acres of woodland. It was the largest continuous woodland area in the National Forest. This large ancient woodland could be traced back to the thirteenth century. Alyssa thought It must contain many secrets but there was not much to go on when considering why the travellers wanted to establish an encampment there. Her history teacher, Mr Hastings may be able to help as he was considered an expert on local history. He was also Toby's uncle. She would phone Toby to see if he would give her his uncle's phone number. This worked out well as Toby had heard about what happened at Jasmine's party and asked if he could come around for a chat. This was the best piece of good news Alyssa had since being grounded and she thought it showed that Toby was still wanting to be her friend. They both arranged that Toby would call her the next day. Alyssa was keen for Toby not to mention that she had phoned him first though! Otherwise, her mother would see this as a way of avoiding her punishment of being grounded for what happened at Jasmine's party.

Toby walked up the drive to Alyssa's house. Suddenly stopped and knocked on the door and stepped back with a frown on his face. He had heard the gossip that was going around about Jasmine and her party. Straight from the horse's mouth. As Jasmine had phoned him straight away. The picture she painted of Alyssa ransacking the lounge and the kitchen, terrorising her pet dog and stealing alcohol before running off into the night seemed a bit extreme. She told him this was a friendly warning to be careful when seeing Alyssa. She did not want him to get hurt. It sounded like she was enjoying herself, despite telling him she wanted to help Alyssa get over this bad patch. Blaming the parents for neglecting her and letting her roam the neighbourhood from an early age. He had briefly met Alyssa's parents and they seemed to be both caring and friendly. Within an hour of Jasmine phoning him, Jess gave him a call. Telling him how brave and friendly Jasmine had been despite having her party ruined. As both phone calls to him had more or less followed each other, he thought Jess had probably been told to do this. She was not a confident girl but one who was desperate to make friends.

Alyssa's mother opened the door. "Hello, Toby! What a surprise, come in."

"Hello, Mrs Durtnall, thank you." Toby paused. "Oh, is Alyssa in?"

"Yes. Alyssa," Jenny shouted, "Toby to see you." She turned to Toby and said. "She has been in a bit of trouble lately and I am sure you will cheer her up. She has been grounded so she can't go out but you are quite welcome to stay!" She smiled. "Would you like a drink and a piece of cake as you have arrived just in time for 'elevenses'."

Toby frowned, what on earth was the woman talking about. "Um yes, I like elevenses they go well with cake."

Jenny Durtnall laughed to see him struggling to be polite.

"Toby, elevenses is the time during the morning when people have a snack. It is an old fashion saying which young people might not have heard of."

Alyssa ran down the stairs and stopped. Both children stared at each other and there was an awkward silence. Jenny turned around glancing at Alyssa as if to say, is your boyfriend trying to get you out of trouble? Before she went into the kitchen to prepare the snack. She was pleased Toby had come around and although she was still punishing her daughter, she did not want her to feel too depressed. Alyssa quickly changed the subject. "Come into the lounge."

"Hi, Liam," said Toby as he walked into the lounge.

Liam looked up. He was sitting at the table finishing off some of his flyers for the cat. "Tobe!" he said before getting back to his work.

Toby wandered over to see what Liam was doing and read the flyer. Liam had also drawn a sketch of the cat. "Sorry to hear about your missing cat, dude," said Toby.

"Oh, it's not our cat. We are trying to find out who owns it as it is always around here. It seems to sleep in our garden shed. The owners must be very worried." Liam knew Toby also lived in the village. "I suppose you have not seen anything?"

Alyssa popped her head around the door holding two cokes. "Come into the garden, Toby." Toby had a quick look at what Liam had written.

PLEASE HELP MISSING CAT SNICKITYLICKERS

We have found a cat she has her name on her red collar

She is friendly and will not scratch. Her name is Snickitylickers

Do you know where she lives? Liam (liam@btinternet.com)

They went and sat on the patio overlooking the garden.

"Thanks for coming. I am sure that you have heard about the party fiasco at Jasmine's?"

Toby smiled. "Yeah, both Jasmine and Jess phoned to tell me. Seems they wanted me to know what a bad girl you are."

Alyssa started fiddling with her can of coke. "I think I have been a bit silly but I am certainly not a thief. I only went to the party to try and improve my friendship with Jasmine. I now wish I had not bothered."

Toby laughed. "They both phoned me within the hour. I think Jess had been told to phone me. All she could talk about was how patient and helpful Jasmine had been despite you wrecking the neighbourhood. Anyway, I like bad girls."

Alyssa smiled and gave Toby a hug and then explained what really happened. "But I did not ask you to come over to discuss the party. I know your uncle, Mr Hastings teaches history at our school and I was wondering if you could give me his phone number. I am doing a project on the history of Groby and Martin Shaw woods and I wanted some information about a traveller community that have lived in this area."

Toby thought for a moment. "OK, I will contact my uncle to see what he thinks. He is manic about all things past. If I give him your phone number, I expect he will be delighted to discuss this with you. His house is just like a library!"

"Great, you're wonderful! I was beginning to feel like I was the most unpopular girl in the district."

Toby blushed and grabbed Alyssa's hand. "You will always have me as a friend." He blushed, spotty cheeks going bright red which made Alyssa laugh.

"Red cheeks and blond hair suits you." Alyssa stood up pulling Toby back into the house. "Now you are here I am hoping Mum will let me out." She glanced furtively at her boyfriend. "I have been grounded for the last week due to the party problems. I am hoping you will be able to give me some freedom."

"Hmm… It will cost you a few kisses." He smirked, then realised what he had said and looked embarrassed.

Alyssa stared into his eyes. Toby was a couple of months older than her and was just beginning to sprout a few hairs on his chin in between the acne! He was also slightly taller and due to his passion for weight training was beginning to lose that chubby-cheeked look. His shoulders and upper body beginning to thicken out. He dressed to show off his efforts. A cameo print parka undone to show off his chest sporting an NYC barcode t-shirt, acid wash skinny jeans and tan Chukka boots. He recently bought some 'Harry Potter' sunglasses. Alyssa thought he was gorgeous but was not going to tell him this. "In your dreams, mate," she whispered. "I will take you down to the woods and tell you a bit about what we found there."

"Hey, that would be cool, thanks!"

"You do sound enthusiastic!"

"Yeah, I don't mind! Getting bored at home at the moment. It's something to do."

"So if you are that keen why not go and see your uncle today and come back tomorrow when we can carry out some research?" She paused. "There will be lots more coke and cake!"

Toby smiled. "OK, it's a deal!"

Alyssa frowned and then smiled. "I think I am having a bright idea," she said. "Come with me!" They both went into the garden where Jenny Durtnall was planting some bedding plants. Alyssa went over and tapped her mother on the shoulder. Gave her a hug.

"Oh, what's that for? Thank you, sweetheart but I have a feeling you are going to ask if you can go out with Toby this morning!"

"Ah!" Alyssa frowned. "Yes, but it is to help me with my studies!"

"Oh, yes?" Jenny Durtnall did not look impressed.

"Look, Mum, at the end of last term I had a conversation with Mr Hastings, you know he is Toby's uncle and he teaches history at school. He told us that if we got bored over the holidays, we could try some historical research in our home town. He would be quite happy to help. So Toby and I would like to do a project on the history of Groby and Raby!" She paused and smiled sweetly at her mother.

"So you want to go out this morning with Toby to see what you can find?"

"Oh, Mum you are so clever how you guessed!"

"Enough of the flattery, young lady but as this is an educational outing, you can go."

Alyssa jumped for joy and was just going to give her mother another hug but Jenny raised both hands in the air. "Hugs are fine but I do not need another one when I'm gardening. You can go on one condition that when you return you will tell me and your father what you have found out."

"Thanks, Mum! Come on, Toby let's go." The children quickly ran back into the house before Jenny Durtnall changed her mind.

Liam sat frowning in the lounge thinking life was not fair as he would have liked to have gone with them, only was told he would have been the 'gooseberry'. Something which he did not understand. Jenny Durtnall stood at the front door watching both children walk off down the street holding hands. She could remember her first boyfriend and the mounting excitement of starting more adult relationships. That tingling in the tummy when you thought about them and the developing problems of having to cope with hormones. "Love young dreams." She sighed.

Liam overheard this and became puzzled. Gooseberries. Dreaming lovers! What on earth was wrong with people today?

Planificare (Planning)

As promised, Toby did contact his uncle who was interested to help Alyssa. After a brief telephone conversation when she told him she was interested in finding more information about the travellers that used to visit Groby and the surrounding area, he sent her information of internet sites to explore like the British Newspaper Archive. He had carried out a small piece of research into the traveller community a couple of years ago when the school admitted two traveller families. But they did not stay long and moved again after a couple of months. He asked Alyssa if he could read the results of her investigations next term. He also suggested that she might like to take history up to a higher level if she was to stay on at school. Having sensed a pupil who was enthusiastic about his pet subject.

Alyssa felt excited. Liam was still keen to print out flyers and circulate them around the village. So far there had been no response, so he was planning on going into the next village, Ratby and due to him now being a model child at home was allowed to do so. This gave Alyssa all the time she needed to carry out her research. When looking at old copies of the Leicester Chronicle, first published in 1792, there was a mention of a small traveller community being driven out of the village as they had parked their caravans on the parish green. The newspaper changed its name to the Leicester Chronicle in 1813 and there were some references to travellers camping in the Martin Shaw woods in 1815. But this time they seemed to have been tolerated by the villagers. So did Liam go back in time when he visited the traveller site last week? She thought it was possible. Alyssa put a tick to the first note on her sheet. The main news was that of the Corn Law dispute with the government. This was a tariff placed on imported food to keep prices high for the farmers. But this meant many poorer families could not afford bread. Three travellers, one older woman and two children were killed when a group of watchmen and constables had dispersed an angry crowd protesting against the Corn Laws in Ratby. There was a short article praising the traveller community for their support and requests were made to find them. They had quickly moved on afterwards and the villagers had collected donations to help them with funeral costs. They were tragically run down by a farmer's wagon when horses panicked when the constables fired warning shots over the heads of the crowd. So Liam was asked to seek justice for the travellers by the old lady? Would this be connected with the deaths in 1815? She remembered the numbers on the wall in the cottage when the lightening flashed before she passed out. Alyssa thought she would send Liam around to St Phillips and St James church in Groby and the Methodist church in Ratby to see if the travellers had been buried locally in the cemeteries.

She then started looking into the magical experiences surrounding gypsy caravans. She read an article on the Gypsy Caravan Dance Company. This company explored the magical energy of dancing together and of honouring the traditions of the past and bringing this back to the present day. The gypsy tribal belly dance gave strength, healing and confidence to those who practised this. Taking them into the spiritual world. Following the actions of the wrestlers so as to solve the problem of opening the cottage door. She also thought following the cat into the first room in the cottage could be considered magical. The picture of a naked man in the tin box found outside the cottage was a 'Mulo', a Gypsy vampire with three fingers on each hand. The parakeets in the caravan had kept shouting the word 'Mulo' when they found themselves in the Romany caravan after their frightening experience in the cottage.

The piece of iron found lying near the tin box would have been worn by those wanting to be protected from vampires who were likely to appear on 'All Hallows Eve'. People would carry hawthorn branches to ward off evil spirits. Alyssa remembered there was a hawthorn branch leaning against the door to the second room in the cottage. She decided this might be useful if they were going to visit the second room in the cottage when they returned. But why were these words being brought to their attention? There must be a reason! She had been gathering information on traveller funerals from a website suggested by Mr Hastings. The travellers were afraid of being haunted by the dead if they had upset the dead person in any way. The Mulo might seek out and haunt the living. Often the grieving family would get an outsider known as a Gorgio to prepare the dead for burial and help the family be at peace again after a death. Many travellers were afraid of touching the corpse. Their possessions would often be buried

74

with them, and this would include any animals. The coffins were therefore huge. It was important for the dead to be returned to their home. Vardo wagons of the dead with their possessions would be burnt. A traveller burial would have many mourners travelling from great distances. When it was not possible for the burial to be at the travellers' homes, there would be 'Hedge Burials' carried out by a few of the mourners. This would be quite a secretive affair where only the close family would know where the body was buried. What seemed to be central to solving this puzzle was the role the cat played. Snickitylickers was responsible for leading Liam to the woods and the gypsy encampment. The cat had helped both Liam with his fight with Jal and Alyssa when she was being attacked by the dog at Jasmine's house. Alyssa ticked off the last question. Liam had thought that the traveller children and their granny were suspicious or afraid of the cat. The cat had led them into the first room in the cottage. They had to keep on trying to get more information as to who owned Snickitylickers if they were going to be able to solve this mystery.

As Alyssa finished checking her notes, Liam trudged into her room and threw himself down on her bed. "I am shattered!" He moaned kicking off his trainers. "Just walked two miles into Raby and have put the fliers of the cat and my sketches of Rawnie and Jal up along the main street. Then walked by the church and stuck some on the lampposts on Stamford Street and Station Road."

"Have you any news from the fliers you put up in Groby yesterday?" asked Alyssa.

"Humph! Nothing, a total waste of time."

"Thanks anyway." Alyssa smiled trying to cheer him up.

"Total waste of time," Liam mumbled going into his bedroom and slamming the door.

However, the next morning he had cheered up. This time rushing into Alyssa's bedroom and jumping on the bed nearly throwing his sister out onto the floor. "Hey, Alyssa, I have had seven emails regarding the fliers about the cat."

Alyssa scratched her head sitting up where she had bumped it on the side of the wall. "Oh, great did you get the addresses of where she was seen? It might be a good idea to plot these on a map of Ratby so as to see what route she took!"

"Yeah, good idea but how come she has been seen in Ratby and not in Groby. Also, nobody has seen Rawnie or Jal, it is as though they never existed!"

Alyssa remained thoughtful. "Hmm! Yes, although it seems the only place the cat has been, is in our house and Jasmine's when she came to help with the dog."

"So you are saying we are the only people that have seen her in Groby? Why?"

Alyssa answered, "Exactly the one-million-dollar question that cannot be answered. Yet!" Alyssa then discussed her research with Liam.

"Wow, do you really think I went back in time when visiting the traveller site last week? Awesome! Yes, and it would explain the strange clothes Rawnie and Jal were wearing!"

Liam went downstairs and asked his father if he could borrow the 'OS' map of the area. His father had many of these to help with his work in the National Forest. He traced out the area where he had placed the fliers and plotted the addresses of those people who had sent him an e-mail. As soon as he had finished, he went upstairs to show his sister. Alyssa studied the map. "Look" – she pointed to the area near St Philip and St James' church – "they are all from people living either to the side or opposite the church."

"So Snickitylickers seemed to have made this her favourite place." Liam was beginning to get excited. "I will send everybody who has replied another message as no one has remembered the dates and times but I would also like to know if this cat entered their houses."

"Good idea, bruv." Alyssa patted Liam on the back. "Now, I am going back to sleep," as she shrank back under the bedclothes.

Later that day, Mr Hastings sent Alyssa a copy of an article he had found in the Leicester Chronicle dated 1841.

Leicester Chronicle 13th November 1841
Travellers slain in protest against the Corn laws.
There was an unhappy situation with much trouble on the village green in Ratby when three gipsies named Patricia Loveridge aged 40 and her two grandchildren Rawnie Love ridge aged 14 and Jal Loveridge aged 9 were knocked down and killed by a horse and cart resulting from riots caused by shots being fired above the crowd by parish constables so as to disperse the crowd in Ratby. Villagers took pity on the distressed and collection was made by the protestors for funeral costs. John Smith parish clerk was the last person to see some travellers pushing a hand cart with the bodies of the deceased. The question now needs to be asked. Where did the travellers go after leaving Ratby?

This cannot be possible, thought Alyssa. She had never seen the children and their granny but Liam had only a few days ago. Liam was also confused.

"Look, I did play with them. I talked to Granny Pat in her caravan. I climbed with Jal up to the treehouse!"

"What about us showing Mr Hastings your sketches of granny Pat and the children? He might be able to tell us if they were with the travellers before they left the area." But then she pulled a face as another idea struck her. "Are you sure, Liam? You know how dreamy you can be, did you just imagine it?"

"Don't be so stupid, how did I know their names. Those names printed in a newspaper one hundred and seventy-six years ago!"

"So it seems the cat wanted you to know about this and she wanted me involved when helping me fight the dog at Jasmine's house. It seems she must have come to Groby to find us." Alyssa's mind was beginning to work overtime. "But why did she also visit Ratby and go near the church?"

Liam stared at his sister as another idea came into his head. "We need to find a map of Ratby in 1841. The village would not look the same as it is today. It might help to find an explanation as to why Snickitylickers visited Ratby."

Mr Hastings gave the children details where they could get copies of old maps from local archives although there was a cost involved. Liam managed to persuade his dad to get them copies of maps, not a difficult task as this fitted nicely with Alyssa's explanation of doing a local history project of the area during the holidays. Anything educational would open the family's treasure chest! Looking at the map, the children noticed the church was still there. Ratby itself was much smaller, just a main street with small houses and cottages on each side. There was a village green to the side of the church. It was much smaller now due to more houses being built. Reading the article in the Leicester Chronicle again of 1841, mention was made of the protest being held at the village green. This was the area where the travellers died. It matched where the cat had been seen by the residents.

"I suppose this could be the reason why the cat was around that area, Liam."

Liam thought for a while. "I suppose Snickitylickers could have been searching for something connected to the riot?"

"Liam, let's have a look at those replies to your fliers from Ratby. There was one person who did put the date when they saw the cat."

Liam switched on his 'iPad'. "Yes, here it is. July 16."

Alyssa looked startled. "We were still in school then! The holidays did not start until July 25, the night I went to Jasmine's house for the sleep in. So maybe the cat was looking for us. Could not find us in Ratby and was searching for over a week until she found us in Groby. It would make sense. She would go to the site of the killings first if she wanted to find some historical attachment or link to the past in 2017."

Alyssa suddenly jumped up as though she realised, she was sitting on a bees nest. Liam surprised, burst out laughing.

"My last telephone call with Mr Hastings." His sister started pacing around the room, ignoring her brother. "We were discussing the traveller community and he asked me about our family's connection with gypsies. He told me that our surname Durtnall had strong links with a Romany community living in a village called Durkynhole in Kent."

Liam looked surprised raising his eyebrows. "Wow, so we could have Romany ancestors!" he gasped.

"I feel we are getting somewhere, Liam. What we need to do now is go back to the cottage."

"Yes, Alyssa, I know what you are thinking. What is in that second room? But before we do that I want to talk to Mr Hastings as he also told me he was involved in discussion with the travellers and the parish council before they left the woods last month."

Mr Hastings was only too pleased to share information about the recent visits of the traveller community to Groby. They had stopped only for a couple of days in Groby and parked their caravans in the woods outside the village. They were on their way to Breedon on the Hill only six miles from Groby but would not explain why they were going there. His description did not match what Liam saw on his first visit. There were only four caravans recently built in 2014. No children were on the site. He had looked at the sketches of granny Pat and the children and had not seen them at the campsite. He found them difficult to talk to. Quite secretive. They did not want to cause any trouble. The only person he was happy with was Tom Loveridge whom he had met at the school a few years ago when Tom admitted his children to Markfield School, but they only stayed a couple of weeks before moving on. However, he had kept in contact with him as he was interested in finding out more about the Romany culture. The result of their meeting was that the Parish Council gave them permission to stay for a week as long as they left the site tidy and did not damage any of the historical trees around Martin Shaw woodland.

Pomana (Death Feast)

On Sunday morning, the children set out for the cottage. Alyssa considered this to be a good day as their parents were busy organising a Sunday Garage Safari in the village where the residents sold unwanted items from their garage drives. Maps were prepared, showing houses that were selling goods and residents charged to have their information put on the map. So James and Jenny Durtnall were happy to let them out for the day. As they were walking to the woods, they were surprised to see Snickitylickers following them. Liam bent down to make a fuss of the cat. She was having nothing to do with him today. The cat ran off ahead of the children and disappeared over the gate and into the field. There were no wagons parked near the woods. The whole area was clear as the children came to the other side of the field and climbed over the fence before walking up the hill. Both were concerned that the cottage would have disappeared as well. They need not have worried. It was still there. The thatched roof had a green sheen caused by the sunlight. The rickety fence had seen better days and was beginning to sag in places. This time, the front door was not locked. It was as if the door remembered them. Liam stopped and looked back at his sister.

"OK, sis, are you ready for this?"

Alyssa, out of breath from trudging up the hill, just nodded. They walked in and immediately smelt damp and rotting vegetation. The first room on the right was open and they both went in rather nervously. Snickitylickers followed them in and jumped up on Alyssa's shoulder and quickly sprang down to the ground and ran out of the door. As if to show them that they were in the wrong room. The children followed the cat who then sat in front of the other room on the left. The Hawthorn branch was still propped up against the door. But the door was locked.

Liam groaned and looked down at the cat. Snickitylickers sniffed at the branch and looked up as if to say pick it up. Liam did so.

"Hawthorn berries during ancient times were used to make medicines and were often called the 'bread and cheese tree'. It was a lifesaver during famines." Alyssa explained. She had carried out some research on the hawthorn tree since seeing it in the cottage on their last visit. "There must be a clue here to help us open that door."

Liam yawned and put some of the leaves and berries into his mouth.

"Hey, Liam, don't be stupid. It will make you sick!"

After a couple of munches, he spat into his hand. Peered at the spittle. "It looks a bit like porridge. It's slimy."

Alyssa tried pushing on the door. "Look, it has smeared some of it on the hinges, it might help to open the door." So both children started chewing leaves and berries until they had enough to smear both hinges. Again, Alyssa pushed the door which slowly opened.

The cat rushed into the room and disappeared. There was that green mist they had seen in the other room with the multicoloured rainbow. But it was very quiet. Unlike the first room. It felt like both children had been wrapped in cling film. There was a gentle pressure they felt inside their heads. As though their brains were floating in cooking oil. Alyssa stumbled outside the room to grab the branch and brought it back into the room. Holding it seemed to help. She felt the energy and quickly ripped off a part of it. Not feeling the thorns that dug into her fingers as she did so. She gave some of the branch to Liam. Holding the branches in front of them seemed to clear the air and lifted the atmosphere around them so that they could both think and see clearly. The cat had disappeared. On the far wall was some old parchment and what looked like a song or a poem on it.

'Whan the turuf is thy tour
And thy pit is thy bour,
Thy fel and thy white throte
Shullen wormes to note
What helpeth thee thenne
Al the worilde wenne?'

"What's that all about then?" Liam scratched his head.

"I am not sure but I will try and remember it as Mr Hastings might have some ideas." Alyssa kept repeating it over and over again until she was satisfied that she had learnt it off by heart.

As the children stared at this piece of parchment, it seemed to drift away into thin air. Both children were expecting flashes of lightening and that awful moaning sound they experienced during their first journey out of the cottage and ending up in Granny Pat's caravan. This time it was a gentle journey. Liam thought travelling through time was a bit like riding a bike. To start with you were always falling off and hurting yourself, but once you got used to it you were able to ride safely.

The wall of the room could no longer be seen. Liam started looking around and saw a church. It had a square tower with a window at the top. There was a path winding up from the street that meandered through a graveyard. It reminded him of somewhere he had been before. "Alyssa," he shouted, "I know where this is! This is Ratby where I put up the fliers the other day. But without the houses on the main street. I think this must be Church Lane. Look!" He pointed to a village Green next to the church. There was a crowd standing and listening to a man that seemed to be shouting and waving his arms about in the air like an excited scarecrow. People were pushing and shoving each other in trying to get closer to the speaker who was standing on an upturned crate. To the side of the crowd were a group of men dressed in black, many with beards and one who was blowing on a whistle. It seemed he was trying to interrupt the speech.

"Liam, over there!" Alyssa pointed to the other side of the crowd and there were the two Vardo caravans they had seen at the gypsy encampment.

"Hey Rawnie, Jal," screamed Liam as he saw the two Romany children sitting with Granny Pat in the front of the crowd. Liam was now pushing his way through the crowd but finding this difficult as to the angry response he was getting. One man grabbed Liam by the collar and slapped him around the head. Then dragged him back and threw him into the gutter. Alyssa screamed and launched herself at the man, her fists and legs punching and kicking, but this only made the man laugh. He pushed Alyssa on top of her brother.

"Parish constables!" shouted somebody from the crowd.

The man glanced over his shoulder looking rather guilty. He walked back into the crowd who were laughing and cheering, clapping him on the back. Suddenly, there were shots fired over the heads of the crowd by the Parish constables. Alyssa sat up, grabbed Liam and checked that he was OK. Both children ducked and rolled out of the way as the crowd started panicking. Women grabbed their babies. Some older people were being trampled on and one old man had his walking stick stamped on and broken by the fleeing horde. Most of the crowd managed to escape. But a horse pulling a cart across the village Green with a poster attached to the cart. 'Corn Laws to go'. The poster was tugged and pulled by the breeze as the horses reared up in front of the three people still sitting in front of the speaker, he jumped off the crate and rolled out of the way. The children and their granny were not so lucky. The front wheel of the cart seemed to catch Granny Pat across her legs, dragging the old lady across the green with one leg crushed between the spokes of the wheel. Both Rawnie and Jal grabbed her arms and were also pulled along behind the cart. Alyssa could see the girls' head bumping across the green. Eventually smashing into the wall at the side of the churchyard in a spray of blood. The driver pulled back on the rains while trying to turn the horses who became confused. He decided to jump off the cart to save himself. The two horses bucked and wrestled with the reigns that had been released by the driver they were confused trying to turn in opposite directions which caused the cart to lean dangerously over balancing on one wheel. Granny Pat held by

86

Jal started twisting and rolling as the cart teetered on the brink of being overturned. A reign snapped not being able to take the strain as the cart turned so as to pivot on one wheel. It seemed to stay in this position for ages. Then suddenly collapsed on top of the boy and his granny with a sickening squelch.

Both Liam and Alyssa sprinted furiously towards the wrecked cart. Liam much faster than his sister as he threw himself down skidding across the grass. But he suddenly jumped up and stared, not wanting to go any farther. The cart was on its side with one wheel smashed completely while the other on the uppermost side of the cart spinning lazily around and around. Stuck between the spokes was a human leg. A body was nowhere to be seen. Alyssa stood behind her brother. She had spotted granny Pat lying like a crumpled and damaged doll on her back a few feet away. The bleeding stump of her right leg sticking up in the air. It looked like a red-hot poker. The other leg just below the knee was clamped between the spokes of the wheel.

"Liam, look under the cart, is Jal under there?" she shouted.

"No, I can't do this!" wailed Liam. He started shaking, tears pouring down his face.

"OK come away and sit down over there behind that bush." Alyssa needed to take Liam's mind off the horror that was in front of them. He needed something to take his mind off things. "Look, sit down here and breathe deeply. Then I want you to go and look for the horses." She glanced behind her and saw the horses slowing to a canter after breaking free from the cart. "I am going to see how granny Pat is." She ran over to where the old lady was lying. Flat on her back, her eyes staring unseeing up into the sky. Alyssa gently grabbed her hand. It was ice cold. The old lady was dead. She looked around to see some of the villagers running towards the cart. *They would take care of things,* she thought. Walking slowly away, now searching for Rawnie. She had seen the girl being pulled along by the cart and being smashed into the wall. She walked over to her. Rawnie lay on her stomach with her head propped up against the wall at a funny angle. She was just about to turn the girl over when somebody grabbed her shoulder pulling her away.

"Nay lass leave her be. Ye dain't needing to see this. She'll be beyond hope. Nah."

She turned to look at the man. He was tall. A workman. He wore a scruffy looking shirt under what looked like a linen tunic with high leather boots. Alyssa thought he looked like a typical peasant from the 1700s. The man led her away from the body and sat down with her on the bank. He seemed nice. He spoke gently to her and asked if she was alright. She noticed he was silently crying.

"What's the matter?" *Rather a silly question*, she thought but wanted to say something so as not to feel awkward.

"My poor Rawnie!" sobbed the man. "Ye see, I am her uncle. We are travellers helping to support the village by this protest march. The corn law has made working on the land difficult for us as well as the villagers here."

Alyssa remembered reading about the Corn Laws in the article she had read in the Leicester Chronicle.

"My name's Lester Loveridge, I am Rawnie and Jal's uncle. Those children and their granny who were knocked down by that cart." He patted Alyssa on the head. "I must see how Jal is." He stumbled over to the wrecked cart. She watched him as he grabbed part of a broken wheel and used the spokes as a lever so that he could get Jal out from under the cart. She watched him turn the boy over and check to see if he was breathing. Standing up, he gasped clenching his hands around his face and wandering around the wreckage wailing in agony. He turned around to look at Alyssa. "What is to become of us, Lassie?" he wailed. "They are all dead, all dead!"

Alyssa went and found Liam who was sitting looking at the horses who had now been taken away by their owner. There was a crowd gathering around the cart. "Liam, they are all dead and their uncle is over there. I think we should try and help them."

The children ran over to the cart. The bodies of Granny Pat and the grandchildren had been wrapped up and placed in a cart that was being pulled by a donkey owned by one of the villagers. As they joined the crowd, they heard people talking about how they could help. As the man started pushing the handcart out of the field and onto the track leading out of Ratby village. Suddenly, he turned around and started shouting at the crowd, some of whom were following him. "Nay, stay back, this is family business, traveller business. Thank you for your concern."

"He has not much money and we should start a collection, after all, they are not from this village but stayed wanting to help us," muttered a woman. She was a big ruddy-faced woman who seemed to be getting rather angry. Shaking her fists at the Parish constables. "You'll pay for this, you villains, shooting 'yer' weapons! Can ye see what you've done? Murderers!" she screamed. This seemed to energise the crowd, some of whom grabbed sticks and farming implements and started walking over to confront the constables who walked quickly off the village Green.

Alyssa took a big breath in trying to hide how nervous she was and asked the woman where the man was going.

"He said he would take 'em' to St Mary and St Hardulph on Breedon on the Hill. I know travellers get on with 'em' nice folks over there. It will be a hedge burial. A holding for the dead until they can be buried according to their ways. He has no money and we have given 'im a spade to dig graves fer now!" She started waving to the traveller. "Hey, Lester, me husband's cart, take it and leave it on the hill by the church. Make sure you hobble the donkey by the church gate, we will pick it up later."

Lester Loveridge waved to show he had heard and jumped onto the cart and slapping the donkey, both were seen making slow progress over the rocky ground and up into the misty hills surrounding Ratby.

"Hey, Alyssa look, isn't that Snickitylickers!" Liam pointed to a cat that had suddenly appeared sitting under a bush, a few feet away from them. Both children ran over to take a closer look. There was a deep rumble and the ground started shaking. Liam tripped and fell into the bush. Alyssa tried to grab him and just managed to grasp his arm. Both somersaulted through the bush and started rolling down a hill. Alyssa, who still was gripping Liam's arm, reached out with her other hand and grabbed part of a fence. This stopped them from falling further. They both looked up and saw a church with a square tower with crenulations across the top. This reminded them of a small castle. It was set right in the middle of a graveyard.

"Alyssa, look, there's that donkey and cart tied by the church gate!" Liam ran over and started stroking the donkey. He was totally ignored and was pushed roughly out of the way as the donkey started munching away at some long grass.

Alyssa went and had a closer look. The cart was empty. "Liam, I think we must be at the church at Breedon on the hill." She looked around and saw a small group of people gathered in a circle on the brow of the hill behind the church. Next to a rickety old fence near the church wall. She could hear sounds of digging and some of the children were crying.

Alyssa and Liam looked at each other. Both were feeling a bit weak and dizzy. Liam suddenly sat down, his legs felt shaky and he felt so tired. Alyssa looked around. They were both sitting on the earth floor of the second room in the cottage. Snickitylickers purring, rubbing herself up against Alyssa's back. Alyssa turned around and grabbed the cat putting it on her lap. "So what do we do now?" The cat jumped off her lap and walked towards the door.

"It looks like we need to go home." Liam smiled. "I am ready for my tea!"

Dat (Father Gets Involved)

Alyssa lay in her bed. She looked at her watch. 9.00 am. *Too early*, she thought and pulled the duvet over her head. She had nothing to do. Liam had been allowed out with friends. She was on her own. How long would it be before her parents started pestering her to get up? I am now a teenager, I need to rest my hormones. Was one response, she was preparing to use if challenged by her dad. He had taken time off work today to help volunteers in the woodland trust. They were digging drainage ditches in the Martin Shaw Woods. He had agreed to meet the group at 11 o'clock by the gate. Just where the gypsy camp had settled a couple of weeks ago. She might go along later. It was a good excuse to find out more information about the woodland as there would be plenty of other people to talk to. Some of them had been working as volunteers before she was born. She felt a bit better now that she had a plan of action. Liam had been eager to share their experiences at the cottage with everybody. She had persuaded him to keep quiet. Nobody would believe him anyway. Particularly as Liam was well known to be living a lot of the time in a world of his own. The cottage seemed to be like a bridge. Going into the rooms took you to different places in the past. Everything was linked to travellers. Their wagon, the parakeets, going back in time to visit the site where the children and their granny were killed by the horse and cart in 1841. She wanted to know who owned it. There was an enchantment to this place. She felt it as soon as she walked through the door. It was a magical place. *OK*, she thought, flinging off the duvet, wandering around the bedroom grabbing some underwear from the drawer, if she was quick her father who was in the kitchen as she could hear him sorting out the dishwasher, she might get breakfast made for her, if she was quick.

Alyssa's dad was delighted to take his daughter to the woods with him. He proudly introduced her to the group. She was given the task of carrying the earth the volunteers were digging to make a trench away in a wheelbarrow and sprinkling it on a flat piece of ground. It was tiring work and soon both her arms and back were aching. She was very grateful when the group decided to stop for lunch. Her father had made sandwiches with his homemade bread. They looked like doorstops as the slices were so thick. Oozing with bacon. Everyone laughed to see them both trying to cram the bread into their mouths. There must have been a whole packet of bacon in each sandwich drenched in tomato ketchup. Maisey one of the volunteers came and sat on the tree trunk next to Alyssa. "Hey, girl that's one mega sarnie you have there. You could feed the whole of China with that 'un." She laughed.

"My dad does not know the meaning of the word 'thin'." Alyssa replied, mopping up some ketchup that had run down her chin.

Maisie laughed taking off her headscarf and scratching her head. "Always wear one of these when working here otherwise, I go home with my hair covered in ants and other such beasties, but it gets so hot once you start working."

Alyssa picked up the scarf which had pictures of thatched cottages printed all over it. "It's a pretty scarf," she said.

"Thank you, lovely, one of my old boyfriends gave it to me. It's easy to wash and the colour don't run so you can put it in the tumble drier."

"Do you know anything about that small cottage just around the corner from these woods?"

Maisie paused, frowning. Then suddenly remembered where it was. "Why yes, I do know something about it. You see my boyfriend was a traveller and his family owned it. The National Trust wanted to buy it but they wouldn't sell it. It is very old! Why have you been snooping around there, young lady?"

"I am doing a history project on the area in my school holidays."

Maisie stared at Alyssa. "Oh, I can think of better things to do with my time!" She paused, "Oops, sorry, I was not very academic when I was at school. When I was younger, me and my friends used to play in it until one day one of my friends, Sally I think, got very scared. She said it was haunted. We went and told the travellers about it and they agreed and told us it was not safe to play there, so we did not go back again! My boyfriend said it was a very important building. Part of their heritage. He told me there was history inside it! Did not really understand what he meant by that though!"

On their way home, Alyssa asked her father about the cottage.

"The traveller cottage, hmm! Yes, that goes back to the seventeenth century. The traveller community spent a lot of money on it a few years ago. They practically rebuilt it using the old methods. You know daub and wattle for the walls. They used branches from Martin Shaw woods for the wattle weaving the thin branches together. The daub was a mixture of clay and limestone and crushed chalk and hay so as to hold the mix together. They then plastered over the wooden frame. They used this to replace a lot of the walls as they were very weak and beginning to crumble. Once they had repaired the wall, they painted them with whitewash. Yes, I went and helped them with the whitewashing. Alyssa, do you know we have links with the traveller community due to our surname being Durtnall!"

Alyssa nodded. She did know about the family connection but did not want to stop her father from talking about it.

"I know a friend of mine also wanted to help but the travellers did not like him being around. So he felt uncomfortable about this and left. They told me he was not related to their community. Only those who had close links with them were allowed to help them rebuild the cottage."

"Why was this, Dad?" she asked.

"Alyssa, travellers are very private people. They are often picked upon by others as their lifestyle is so different. They knew that my family used to live in Kent in the village of Brasted near Westerham and my family founded a building company in 1591. R. Durtnall and Sons from Brasted. The travellers knew about this. They have copies of newspaper articles tracing their family history. They were known as 'upright' people who were not afraid of a challenge. This is why they are now recognised as the oldest builders in Britain."

"Dad, when you were helping with the cottage, did you see any ghosts?"

Her dad laughed. "No, I was too busy with the whitewash to think about that. But later, when the cottage was finished, they did invite me back for a party and drinks. There were so many people there not everyone could get into the cottage. Travellers have large families, my friend, Tom Loveridge had ten children, his eldest daughter was getting married the next week and they were spending their honeymoon in the cottage."

"How old was she?"

"Hmm! I think she was 16!"

"Wow, that was young. Would you let me get married when I am 16?"

"Certainly not. I think that is too young. But not according to the traveller community as this is one way the girls can leave their home, otherwise parents would keep them to help with the family."

Her dad suddenly stopped walking. "Oh although I did not see any ghosts, I must admit to feeling a bit strange, but I thought it was me drinking too much!"

Alyssa grabbed her dad's hand as they continued to walk home together. "Dad, Liam and myself have been inside the cottage and something very strange happened. Liam has met some of the travellers a few weeks ago." She paused and took a deep breath, not knowing how her father would react to this piece of news. She was expecting to be told off but her father remained very quiet.

"Let's sit down here for a minute and you can tell me all the details," he said, sighing as he did so. It was as though he was expecting this piece of news.

Alyssa sat down, thinking quickly, she did not want to tell the truth. It was really unbelievable what had happened so far, but what she could do was adapt a story that would be accepted by her father so he might be able to help. So, she started talking about the information that Toby's uncle sent her. Explaining the death of the travellers in the riots held in Raby against the Corn Laws in 1841. Adding that the last piece of evidence was the bodies being taken out of the village and were last seen in Breedon on the Hill near the church of St Mary and St Hardulph.

Her father listened carefully. Scratching his head as he remembered a conversation he had with her history teacher two years ago at a parents open evening at the school. It was the time the school had admitted a traveller family which started them talking about their surname being recognised by Mr Hastings as having a link to the traveller community. He carried out some research of his own and was aware of the killings during the riots. He told her that there was no evidence to show a proper burial had been carried out. The travellers that had attended the school only stayed for a couple of weeks before moving on and they did not leave a forwarding address. So he decided to contact Tom Loveridge as they had exchanged contact details a month ago when the travellers had stayed in the village for a couple of nights. It was about time he spent some time in helping his daughter with her school project.

Divano (Meeting or Discussion)

It was a couple of weeks before Alyssa's father had heard from his traveller friend. Tom Loveridge. Arrangements were made for a meeting at the cottage in two days' time as the travellers were returning to Oxford where they were staying at a licensed site which they called home.

The school holidays were coming to an end and both Alyssa and Liam were keen to visit the cottage again. They had kept away as they did not want to upset parents or the travellers. It was the end of August on a bright and sunny day when the children and their father waited for Tom Loveridge and his wife. Their mother, Jenny was at school preparing for the new term. The traveller family had gone back to Oxford already. Tom Loveridge and his wife Gene had come to the cottage. As soon as Alyssa and Liam saw Tom, they were both struck by how much he looked like the person they had met in Ratby in 1841. Lester Loveridge, Rawnie and Jal's uncle. He invited them into the cottage. Both children noticed he had a key which was used to open the door. This was certainly not there on their last visit. The cottage had not changed much except it was very tidy. The earthen floors still had a musty smell inside. They all went into the first room on the left. This now had tables and chairs that were covered with plastic sheets to stop mould staining the furniture. These were removed and everybody sat down. Alyssa looking around nervously. The first time they went into this room there were swirling green mists hanging around and flashes of lightening. She glanced over at Liam who was also looking rather worried.

Tom introduced his wife, Gene. They were both dressed like hitch hikers in jeans and waterproof jackets. Both covered in rings and studs. Gene with two large silver plaited earrings dangling from her ears that seemed to be continually swinging to and fro as she settled herself down on the chair. Liam seemed to be mesmerised by them and a quick kick from Alyssa brought him back into the real world. Tom Loveridge had a pin stud in his nose and in his ear. They were green and seemed to sparkle when a ray of light shone through the small window at the back of the house. He had the letters G-E-N-E tattooed one letter on the top of each finger.

"Welcome to the cottage of dreams folks. Good to see yer all."

Gene nodded her head. She was built more like a scrum half in Rugby. Her arms looked powerful and she sat forward on the chair grasping her knees with her hands. Orange nail varnish seemed to match the lipstick she was wearing. "Peace to all, peace to all." She nodded and then winked at Liam who became quite embarrassed and started fidgeting on his chair staring at the mud encrusted floor.

Alyssa's father took out a hip flask containing whisky and passed it to the travellers who both took a large swallow before passing it to Alyssa. She quickly gave it back to her father before Liam could grab it!

"Ashen Devlesa Romale," replied Gene giving a 'thumbs up' before smacking her lips together.

"May you remain with God." Tom quickly translated.

The two travellers listened intensely when their father repeated what Alyssa had told him when walking home from working in Markfield woods together the other night. The couple had a good knowledge of their history and seemed quite excited on hearing where the bodies of the dead children and their grandmother were last seen in Breedon on the hill. As this fact was not printed in the newspaper. It was witnessed by Alyssa and Liam when they had been taken back through time.

"That's why we came down this way earlier to visit Breedon to see if there was any sign of a hedge burial," he said. "You see, we do not keep records and information is passed down by talking to the family members. This keeps things secret from the public. We dinna want them meddling in our business."

"Tom do you think they were buried up in Breedon?" said their father.

"We know only Lester stayed with the handcart while the rest of the family scattered and left the village. Now Lester would have only been able to make a shallow grave so as to start a Hedge Burial, quickly carried out when a community is travelling from one site to another. Ye see, the dead would not be taken with 'em for fear of evil spirits attacking members of the family like, who might have been unkind to the deceased during their lifetime. They would be afraid of the Mulo, a sort of vampire, or medium capable of reaching the world of the dead following them." Tom paused and sighed, sadly looking around the group. "Lester would have been looking for a church high on a hill, somewhere remote see! We think Breedon church would be a good match!"

Liam had stopped fidgeting on his chair and was beginning to look quite pale. Alyssa put her hands on his shoulders and gave him a quick hug which he did not appreciate, shrugging his shoulders and moving away from his sister. But at least it brought some colour back into his cheeks.

James Dartnell took a swig from the whisky flask passing it around again as he knew both liked whisky and would be encouraged to talk after having another drink. "So, if there has not been a proper burial maybe there should be one? Look back in 2012 when the remains of Richard third were found in a Leicester car park, he was buried again. What was good for him should be good for your family, Tom. Gene, what do you think?"

Gene's eyes lit up and she started to smile. "Aye, that would be justice."

"Slow down there! Whoa, woman!" Tom glared at his wife. "We dinna want everybody knowing our business, eh! Hedge burials should only be known by the family."

"So, yer idiot! Are ye going to sacrifice justice for the sake of tradition?" Gene stood up knocking over the chair and Tom quickly stood facing her. James Durtnall quickly stepped between them and by this time, Liam was ready to run out of the room until Alyssa grabbed him and held him against the wall. Having his sister near him seemed to calm him down.

The two travellers grabbed the chairs and sat down again. Tom banging his chair legs down on the floor.

James gratefully glanced over to Alyssa and nodded to say thank you for looking after Liam. "It's OK, kids, come and sit back down again. Oh, I forgot." He took two packs of blackcurrant juice drinks out of his jacket, both children ran over and grabbed them from their father. Alyssa sat back down again and managed to stop herself from giggling when Gene grabbed Liam roughly sitting him on her knee. He was so shocked, he kept very still with a red face quickly stuffing the straw from his drink into his mouth.

"Aye, ye ah a sweet lad."

"Thanks." Liam suddenly wiggled off her lap and went back to his corner keeping well out of everybody's way.

"I have an idea that both of you might like to think about!" said James. "The Church St Mary and St Hardulph, Breedon on the hill is always struggling for funds. They need to renovate the church by replacing some of the church's roofs. If I went to see them and suggested I paid for a digger to do some excavating around the church site to look for their remains. If we find any, you hold a traditional burial. This would be a good promotion for the church which then could attract tourists. Donations could then be paid back to me for the cost of excavation and the rest could help pay for the roof. What do you think?"

Tom started pacing around the room. "A traditional burial would require a Varnon Wagon. A Romany Wagon. The bones would be placed in a coffin. There would be nothing else though as all their belongings would have disappeared years ago. They then would be burnt."

"Hey," shouted Gene making Liam jump. "We have the Reading Wagon in one of our fields near Oxford, it could be painted up. It'll look grand! You dinna need to worry about the burial site being open to all. What we do is take the ashes

103

and bury them nearby. With only close family being present. Nobody else will know where that is."

Tom stopped pacing and stared at his wife. "Hey, that's grand! It might just work." He seemed to have forgotten about his desire for a private burial in the excitement of getting a proper burial ceremony arranged. "Then folk would remember us, eh! Good plan, good plan, James!"

James also was beginning to get excited. "Yes, and the site where the burning took place could be used as a permanent place to celebrate the finding of the remains. Just like what happened with Richard 3rd!"

After that, everybody seemed happy. There were hugs and handshakes all around. Before they left the cottage, James and Tom agreed on a date to go and see the local vicar of St Mary's and St Hardulph. As they were leaving, he turned around and said. "If it was not for my children, this would never have happened. We all need to thank them for all of their hard work, both have given up their holiday for this!"

"If we are successful, we will celebrate in true traveller fashion." Gene smiled at both children, patting Liam on the head and smiling at Alyssa. "These two will be the stars of the show!"

Istoria Bisericii
(Church History)

The new school term had started and Mr Durtnall was busy at work so it was two weeks later before he managed to see the local vicar. He asked Tom Loveridge to come with him and the Vicar Percy Taplet invited them over for tea and cakes on a Sunday afternoon. Liam on hearing this was desperate to go as well. He had heard the Vicar's Wife Kiona was a great cook who made ice cream cakes for his friend Jax who's cousin lived in the village. Alyssa hearing of this also did not want to be left out. So the children pestered their father constantly during the week until he finally admitted that taking them might help their cause as he had heard that Mrs Taplet adored children. Jenny Durtnall was determined to come along despite her busy schedule. She decided she needed a break from pupils' 'SAT' results and lesson planning.

So, on the Sunday, they all drove over to the church. Nobody apart from Tom had been to the village before and were shocked when they first saw the church from the car situated so high up above a quarry. However, when they got to the top of the hill the views were stunning. The vicar lived down in the village but he wanted them to see the church. They could then explain to him how much they wanted to dig so as to try and find the remains of the travellers. Alyssa gasped as she saw a donkey tethered to the church gate post. So did Liam as they remembered there was a donkey pulling the cart on their last visit in 1841. They could remember the lady in the crowd telling Lester Loveridge to tie the donkey to the gatepost when he had buried the bodies and they would pick the animal up later.

"Hey, are we back in 1841 then?"

Liam's dad turned to stare at Liam. "What are you talking about, Liam?"

"Oh nothing, Dad." He started blushing in embarrassment.

"Liam, shut the door," whispered Jenny Durtnall giving her son a hug.

"Get off me!" Liam shouted, running off ahead of the group which made everyone laugh.

"Dad! Liam and I were talking about what this area would look like hundreds of years ago, last night before we went to bed." Alyssa glared at Liam.

A man dressed in a black habit and wearing the traditional white dog collar walked down the path to meet them, waving frantically. Percy Taplet, local vicar and a jolly eccentric gentleman. To Liam, he looked very old and a bit shaky on his feet. "Friar Tuck," muttered Liam who started giggling but soon stopped when Alyssa jabbed him in the ribs.

"Hello, hello, folks. You must be the Durtnall's?" He stopped to stare intensely at everybody. He pointed at Liam. "You must be Horace? Oh no." He paused. "That was yesterday when I met a Horace. Beastly child, called me a fat monk. Rude boy!"

Liam stepped forward. "My name is Liam, pleased to meet you. Are we going to have some of your wife's cakes?"

"Liam, don't be so rude," shouted Alyssa.

Liam just glanced and shrugged his shoulders.

Once everyone had introduced themselves, the vicar started muttering to himself. Everybody stood in an embarrassed silence. "Hmm yes, oh, sorry. I will tell you about this lovely church. Did you know this is the most important church in the two counties because of the Saxon carvings? Oh, yes, indeed. Oh, did you know it was built on a limestone hill? They are mining the limestone, do you see! A shame! Yes, a great shame but gives jobs to the locals, eh? Ha! There was a monastery here at one time. The Danes smashed it to bits. Oh, yes. But King Edgar! Yes, it was Edgar. Do you know he was the first king of England? Gave the church to Aethelwold. Do you know he was a Bishop? Oh yes, he was." He then paused in thought.

Liam was tempted to shout out, "Oh no, he wasn't in true pantomime style."

"Oh yes, where was I?"

"You were talking about Bishop Aethelwold." Alyssa was trying to be helpful.

"Hmm, oh yes, thank you, Anne, oh no, Alyssa! Yeah, got it! Hmm! Aethelwold was given the land by the king and he repaired it. Good man, eh!"

Seeing that the old man was taking another breath to start talking again, Liam jumped into the silence and said, "Why is there a donkey tied to the gate post?"

"Is there? Ah, of course, that's my donkey, he lives up here. There is a barn around the back and he is very useful for the Nativity Play every year."

Everybody heaved a sigh of relief as this prompted the vicar to ask them about the digging they wanted to do. Both Alyssa and Liam had been there before and could remember where they saw Lester Loveridge digging and where his family was standing but they could not explain this unless they had another excuse. Alyssa had one. "I remember reading in one of the old news sheets in 1841 that the donkey and cart were found tied to the gate. I think they would not have been able to carry the bodies far. What do you think, Mum?"

"Yes, I think you are right, Alyssa."

Tom Loveridge agreed. "Yeah, a hedge burial would be somewhere near a bank or even a hedge," he said looking around. "But of course things have changed over the years. But they would not have gone far."

"So, we would want to excavate a few shallow pits in this area by the wall. The other side of the graveyard as we would not want to damage anything." James Durtnall paced out a few rectangular patches about two metres by one metre. "Would that be OK, Vicar?"

"Oh yes, and in fact, you could do a few more if you would like. The managing director of the quarry has agreed to pay for signage so as to identify the burial area."

The vicar quickly clapped his hands and grabbed the donkey.

"Come along, Horace, time you went back to the barn." He turned to face everybody. "Now, off you go and I will see you at the vicarage. It's over there. You can see it from here. My wife is heavily armed with ice cream cake, Liam."

They spent a very happy hour at the vicarage munching cakes and drinking ginger beer. Mrs Taplett the vicar's wife looked younger than her husband and was dressed very much like a character from the 1950s wearing a flowery dress covered in flour and ice cream! The vicar told them he would raise the matter at the next parish meeting which would be in a month's time. It would be quite a delicate matter as the council had just turned down a proposed plan for 72 executive homes in Lime Fields off Worthington Lane much to the villagers' joy. They had formed their own protest group which made Alyssa think of the protest march that went so badly wrong in Ratby all those years ago.

"I will let you know the outcome. I don't think there will be much of a problem as the church has much to gain from the publicity and so has the village. Also, you have clearly shown after the digging has been completed everything will be put back as it should be!" said Kiona Taplet.

September seemed to fly by and in October, Mr Durtnall received a phone call from Vicar Taplet giving them the go-ahead for the minor excavations in Breedon on the Hill. A quick phone call to Tom and arrangements were made to meet outside the church on a Tuesday as this was the quietest day with no other organisations like the Women's Guild using the church. Alyssa had spoken about this to Mr Hastings in school who was also keen to be involved. He remembered Tom Loveridge from years back when his children attended the school for a couple of weeks. He had kept in touch sending Tom copies of old newspapers if they had any news about travellers passing through Leicester, so Tom was happy for him to come along. Word had spread in school about the possibility of finding traveller remains near the churchyard. Alyssa and Liam suddenly became very popular. Liam was beginning to get a bit cocky in telling his story. Jess was in awe of Alyssa. She kept following her around like an excited little puppy. Jasmine however was secretly fuming and kept very quiet and out of everyone's way.

Mr Hastings had asked the headteacher if he could have that Tuesday off school as his archaeological skills would be needed when labelling objects they might find on the dig. He even managed to persuade the school governors to let Liam and Alyssa join the team and miss school for that day. That was on the condition that they both worked on an article explaining the dig for the local newspaper. So the date was set for a possible burial was October 31. Halloween. The dig would start one month before this at the end of September. James and the other adults would start the excavations. Then if human remains were found it gave them a month to get them authenticated ready for the burial. Tom Loveridge could not have been happier. He had found and repaired the Vardo giving it a coat of paint and repaired the front wheel axel. Gene had set to on the inside of the wagon oiling and polishing the carvings of birds, lions, griffins and flowers which showed aspects of Romany culture. The wood-burning stove and chimney Stack was removed, cleaned with a wire brush and put back in its place.

When hearing the wagon would be burnt Mr Hastings was very upset that something of great value and heritage would be destroyed by burning it later. His many attempts to try and persuade Tom to change his mind were not successful. The two nearly came to blows at a meeting held in James's house. This was not helped by Liam getting excited and shouting out FIGHT, FIGHT! One look from his father soon stopped him in his tracks and he then quietly crept upstairs to bed. Alyssa started skipping around the room chanting the poetry she found in the second room in the cottage. Mr Hastings had traced this song which had recently been recorded by the 'mediaeval Babes and he had played this to Alyssa. She knew this off by heart.

'Whan the turuf is thy tour
And thy pit is thy bour,
Thy fel and thy white throte
Shullen wormes to note
What helpeth thee thenne
Al the worilde wenne?

Mr Hastings laughed and started clapping. Tom who also recognised the tune took out his harmonica and started gently playing the melody. Even James started tapping his feet on the floor. But was not moving any other part of his body! Everybody thought this was hilarious and Jenny Durtnall was laughing so much, she suddenly felt very faint and had to leave the room.

"So Alyssa," gasped Mr Hastings. "Can you explain what this mediaeval ballad means?"

"Oh, yes, it is a song about death and people being eaten up by worms. So, I think instead of being miserable at funerals we should be remembering the good times."

"Well, it is rather a morbid song and what it is really saying when we die there will be no more pleasures! In those days, the church was very much into everybody keeping to the church rules." John Hastings laughed. "But I like your interpretation Alyssa better than mine. I will make sure, I bring along the CD and we can play it before burning the van."

"Yes, that is if we find anything," said James, "if we don't then there is not much point, is there?"

With that sobering remark, everybody said goodnight and went home.

Sapat (Digging)

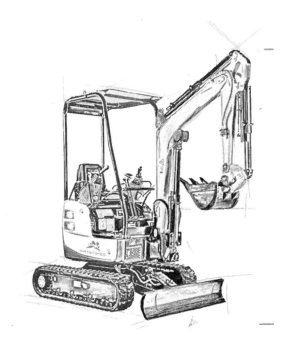

Everything went according to plan. On September 20, James
picked up the digger, a one and a half-ton machine on the back

of a truck. He paid the £90 fee for two days hire. Tom Loveridge had managed to find a truck and trailer that saved him some money. They drove the truck and parked it just outside Markfield woods. James had been given permission to dig in these woods. The woodland trust was draining this part of the woods to encourage the growth of silver birch trees. Both men spent the whole day practising. It took James a long time to master the machine with Tom, shouting out instructions as he guided him around rough bits of ground. At one stage going over a severe steep slope, the digger nearly turned over onto Tom who had to dive out of the way and landed on his back in a particularly rough and spiky hawthorn bush. But both men were satisfied, they could not get any better. Tom would drive the truck and digger up to St Mary's and St Hardulph by 8 o'clock the next morning when the fun would really start.

The next morning, James and Jenny could not believe their eyes when they came downstairs to see both their children waiting by the front door with coats on and rucksacks packed with food.

"Well, this is certainly a first seeing you two ready to go at" – Jenny looked at her watch – "7.30 in the morning!"

"You will now just have to wait!" grumbled James, as he was not in a good mood and was feeling stiff from strained muscles from driving the digger in the woods. "Somebody should have told me it was going to be so difficult, if I had known I would have hired it for another day so I could have had a rest!"

"Hey Dad, I will drive it then?" Liam knew this would not be allowed and just wanted to see the look on his father's face.

"In your dreams, sunshine," muttered James.

Jenny who was always the first out of the house in the morning as she preferred to get to school early to prepare for the day, gave everybody a hug and a kiss and wished them good luck. "And you two, behave and don't get in anybody's way," she shouted as she went out of the door.

"I suppose Mum meant you two." Laughed Alyssa, pointing at her father and Liam.

The weather had turned damp and misty by the time everybody had arrived at Breedon on the Hill. Vicar Taplet arrived puffing and blowing just to wish them luck. He was not the outdoor type and excused himself saying that he had a sermon to prepare.

"Today, St Hardulph is here watching over the whole efforts of your good selves. Hmm, do you know he was a hermit living in Leicester? Yes, yes. A Catholic church was dedicated in his honour. Did you know that? Eh!"

There was a shocked silence broken by Alyssa and Liam roaring with laughter so that Liam fell over on his back grabbing at his knees and rolling into a ball.

The vicar totally ignored Liam but turned around and spoke to the adults. "Ah, but in 1539, the church was taken over by the protestant state. Henry VIII and all that. Hmm, a good move for us, good move for us." As he went off waving at them as he trundled down the hill to his vicarage. No doubt looking forward to a nice, warm building where he could sit in peace and smoke his pipe.

"OK, let's make a start," said James Durtnall jumping up onto the trailer and getting into the digger. It started first time with lots of smoke. Tom unbolted the back of the trailer and slid the ramp down so that James could drive the digger onto the ground.

"Well done, James," shouted Tom, "you haven't hit anything yet!" He laughed.

Before James could make a rude comment, Alyssa pointed over the brow of the hill. "Dad," she shouted, "the Leicester Chronicle said the donkey was left tied to the church gate. There was a small group standing digging over the brow of the hill so I suggest we go over there." She started walking with Liam scampering after her.

Mr Hastings walked over carrying his trowel and other equipment for recording anything they found. He stared at Alyssa in a rather mysterious way, raising his eyebrows. "Alyssa," he whispered, "I would like to talk to you in private later, please."

"What did he say?" asked Liam.

"Oh, nothing don't worry about it!" But somehow, she was worried. Very worried.

James Durtnall made a better job of both driving the digger and operating the machinery. He was still guided by Tom Loveridge. They dug four trenches and Mr Hastings down on his knees with spade and trowel and his collecting bags gave instructions to the children on what to do. He gave them some paintbrushes of various lengths. Some with strong bristles and others with finer bristles.

"So first gently scrape away the soil with the hard brushes until you find something more solid. Then start brushing with the finer brush so that you do not damage whatever it is you are working on."

They worked for two hours without a break with little result. Liam had found a small piece of clay that Mr Hastings thought might be part of an Anglo-Saxon pot. It was friable and course and could have been part of a burial urn. The

Saxons used these for cremated remains. This was placed carefully in a collecting bag and would be taken later to the local museum.

James called everyone over for a break and handed out hot coffee and tea from his rucksack and chew bars to replenish energy levels. They had been working right on the edge of the hill with a steep drop below into the quarry. Tom Loveridge walked over to the edge and stared down below. "Do you think we are looking in the correct place? They have been mining the limestone in this area for a few years now. Due to this, the Church now finds itself right on the edge of this hill. This would not have been the case back in 1841. It would have been a much gentler slope up to the church."

"Tom, yes, that would be correct," replied Mr Hastings. "But does this mean any human remains that were buried here would have been destroyed when excavating the limestone?" There was silence as everyone thought about this.

"I think I will go down to the quarry to see if they had found anything. If human remains were found, they would have had to report it to the local authority. I know they use dynamite to blow out sections of rock after taking off the topsoil and then use heavy diggers, I think they call them D8's. They are very powerful machines to gather up and drop the rocks into smaller pieces. I think finding any human remains from this method are remote." Mr Hastings started walking to his car. "Oh!" He turned around and shouted back, "I will also go and visit the library. I have special access to the local archives and will see if anything has been reported since the quarrying started."

"Things don't look too promising, kids," said their father. "I think we might have to prepare for the worst!"

Liam suddenly jumped up, shouting and pointing to the wall surrounding the graveyard. "Hey, there's Snickitylickers! I am sure I saw her jump over the wall."

The two men looked puzzled.

"Dad, Snickitylickers is the cat we told you about," explained Alyssa, starting to get a bit cross. "Don't you remember Liam making those fliers when we thought we had lost her?"

James Durtnall scratched his head. "Oh yes, the cat. Perhaps she lives up here then!"

Both children rushed through the gate and saw the cat sitting just the other side of the wall near where they had been digging the trenches. "Liam," whispered Alyssa, "do you remember when we were here before and saw the donkey tethered to the church gate, there wasn't a wall here. There was a rickety old fence. None of these graves were here! Wait! Look!" Alyssa pointed at the cat that was walking slowly in that rather jaunty style of hers, stopping to turn and make sure the children were still following her.

"Alyssa, I think she is trying to show us where the graves have been dug. Come on."

So they both followed the cat as it made its way around to the back of the church. Jumping back over the wall and sitting in a small copse of hawthorn bushes, where she started to clean herself. The children ran over to her, Alyssa picking her up and giving her a cuddle. The cat immediately started purring and kneading its claws into Alyssa's jumper. Liam came over to give the cat a stroke.

"Hi beautiful, we have missed you."

"I think we should start digging here, the land has not been affected by quarrying! Let's get Dad to bring the digger over here."

But there was a problem as they could not get the digger over the wall.

It was decided to wait for Mr Hastings to return with any information from the quarry and the museum. James sent him a text saying they would stop for the day and return tomorrow, this would give him extra time to carry out a thorough search for any information in the museum. Alyssa was glad as it meant she would not have to have that conversation with Mr Hastings later that day.

"So Liam and Alyssa, I think I will take you back to school. So you can catch up with your schoolwork," muttered their father.

"What!" Both children looked horrified.

Before they could speak, their father continued, "That is if you want to return with us tomorrow? Remember, the school has only given you one day's leave. Now, if I get you back for these afternoon lessons with a promise you will catch up with the lessons missed over the weekend, your headteacher might let you come back tomorrow."

"OK, Dad, sounds like a plan," said Alyssa. But Liam just pouted and started kicking the ground. He was not a happy bunny at the moment.

His father noticed this. "Liam, make sure you work your socks off, do you hear me?"

Liam held up his hands. "OK, Dad, I surrender."

Everybody laughed.

James Durtnall's plan worked and the children were given another day but both came home loaded with work and they were not looking forward to the weekend.

They arrived back on the hill early the next day before 9 o'clock. James quickly leapt up into the cabin, started the engine and drove onto the field. He suddenly stopped and shouted to the others. "Everybody go and stay by the wall and don't move until I tell you to." With some skidding of tyres, the digger was driven around the back of the church away from the brow of the hill and there was a large bang and stones from the wall were seen flying up in the air.

"What the hell is going on?" shouted Tom, running around to look at the digger. The children went with him; they needed no encouragement to break the rules. James Durtnall was sitting in the digger that had ploughed through a small section of the wall with a smile on his face.

"O dear, my mistake!" He laughed. "I think I need a bit more practice!"

Tom Loveridge started laughing. "Nice one, son, this now solves the problem of getting the digger to the other side of the wall."

"It shouldn't take us long to rebuild the section at the end of the day. After all, I have had a lot of experience of building these dry-stone walls."

"Thanks, Tom. I knew you would not let us down." James winked at his two children.

"Hey Dad, that was cool," shouted Liam clapping his hands.

"OK, children, it is up to you now. Where shall we start digging?"

The children lead the way across the graveyard much nearer the church. Alyssa could remember there were not many graves here in 1841 and a small group gathered in a circle next to the church, there was a sound of digging and earth being thrown up in the air. One of the little girls was running around the back of the circle gathering up the grass turf and putting it neatly by the church wall. Alyssa turned to speak to Liam. "I think it was about here, Liam?" Liam just nodded and stood staring at the ground with his hands in his pockets. Alyssa sighed as she realised, he had no idea where the correct place would be.

James gunned the digger into life and started to dig out two small trenches being careful not to touch any of the old gravestones nearby. The children and Tom started using the plastic collecting bags and the different sizes of paintbrush to dust down any relic they found. They left them in a neat pile by the church. Mr Hastings was teaching that morning but told them he would come up early afternoon. By 11 o'clock, they had not found much in the two trenches so James dug a bit deeper, taking off another couple of metres of soil and then starting two more trenches so as to make a square. When Liam jumped into these trenches he had to be pulled out each time he wanted to move to another trench. By mid-afternoon, he was filthy, covered in mud which seemed to have stuck to his hair, nose and ears.

"Liam, you look like a 'bog monster'." Laughed Alyssa and quickly ducked as a flying turf came whizzing out of the trench narrowly missing her head. She grabbed a handful of earth and ran to tip it over Liam's head but stopped when she saw Mr Hastings walking across the graveyard.

"How are things going?" he asked, going immediately to the collecting bags and started listing the contents.

Mr Harding's Notes (All to be checked with archivist in Leicester Museum.)

1800-Victorian Era

1- Part of a Victorian sink

2- Small part of a cooking range with the word MAG was surprised with this find as it seemed to suggest this was a Magee Range made in Boston USA!

3- Omelette panhandle

4- Part of a Gridiron

5- Small wheel (could have been the back wheel of a penny-farthing.)

6- Three wooden posts 1900 onwards

7- Part of trowel handle

8- bicycle pedal

9- Part of child's toy plastic

10- 20p piece

11- Part of teacup age unknown!

12- Lego figure

13- Candle stub.

He looked up once he had finished and came over to where the others were working. "Hi James, Tom, can I discuss what I have found out about the quarry and the museum?"

"Good idea, Mr Hastings," said James clapping his hands and herding everybody out of the trenches. "Let's all sit down and have a break. Tom, can you start a brew?" He rummaged in his rucksack. "Ah yes, sweets. Thought I had some for everybody." He felt a bit embarrassed calling John Hastings by his surname.

Liam and Alyssa quickly grabbed their packets ripping them open and making everybody laugh.

"There was a time when I could get excited like that!" said Mr Hastings. "Must be getting old!" He glanced around, seeing everybody was waiting expectantly. "Right! I managed to talk to the manager of the quarry a Mr Deadlock who had been there for ten years. We looked up the annual reports about the quarry, but these only went back seven years. He said he has never found any human remains. The only bones that had been identified were cats, dogs and wild animals, foxes and badgers. But not human remains I am afraid. My trip to the museum was more helpful. We know that the villagers collected a burial fund for the travellers. There was an article in the Leicester Chronicle in 1841 describing this and asking what had happened to the money as the travellers had left the area. In 1842 there was another article saying the villagers had used the money to build a memorial in the area they thought the bodies had been buried. This was placed at the back of the church."

"Aye, it sounds right," said Tom. "They would not have been buried at the front for fear of the grave being desecrated."

"Hey, there's Snickitylickers, Look, she has jumped into the last trench," shouted Liam jumping up and down as though there was something wriggling in his trousers. He jumped down into the trench to take her out but as soon as she was put on the grass, jumped back in again.

"Do you think the cat is trying to tell us something?" said Tom. "This cat I have seen around our cottage near Martin

Shaw Woods." He scratched his head. "Wonder if she is a Gorgio?"

"Oh yes, I know what that is!" Alyssa getting really excited. "Now that is an outsider asked to come in to help with a Romany burial as the family do not like preparing the body as they think they might be cursed!" She paused looking at Tom. "Oops sorry, Tom! Did not want to offend your family!"

"Nay lass, good on yer for knowing something about traveller culture, eh!" He looked both at James and John Harding. "Well, we are not getting anywhere here, are we? Why not dig this trench a bit deeper!"

As James was getting ready to start the digger, John Harding asked him to stop. "James, can we wait a minute? Rather than using the digger, let's do some gentle digging with the spades. If there are human remains down there, they could easily be destroyed and missed, with you using the digger and the shovel."

So they all jumped into the pit. The cat on seeing this climbed out and ran off.

John Hastings directed operations. He had the children on each side of the trench using spades chipping away at the surface. He walked in front facing them and collecting anything of importance in his collecting bags.

Then it was James and Tom together doing the same thing.

James scooped out another layer using the digger. Tipping what was in the bucket back into the trench where it was gently broken up into smaller parts. This took ages and it was very tiring as it meant when they were not digging together, they had to get out of the trench to make room for the next two. The only one who stayed in the trench was Mr Hastings.

"It's OK for him!" moaned Liam. "He gets the easy job!"

There was a shout from the trench and the children peered over it to find the two men getting quite excited. It looked like there were some small bones being unearthed. John Hastings told the children to not get back into the trench and asked the two men to get out.

"OK, this is where we have to stop and cover the top of the trench with plastic. There are various health risks associated with handling human remains. Also, we could contaminate the bones by touching them. I told the archaeological trust officer at the museum I would contact him if we found any evidence. He has a friend who is a forensic anthropologist who is also an amateur history buff. He also attends St Mary and St Hardulph church and is a member of the church choir. I am sure he will be able to persuade the vicar for more extensive digging over the next few weeks."

"Mr Harding, what is a phonetic antroplist?" asked Liam.

This made everybody laugh much to his embarrassment and he was about to run off when Mr Hastings patted his head. "Liam, what a great question as I expect everyone would like to know the answer. They are people who understand skeletons very well. From samples of bones found in the earth, they will examine them to try and find the age at death, what race they belonged to, their height and whether they were a man or a woman. They can also tell whether bones are animal or human."

"This will be rather expensive, Mr Hastings!" James frowned. "Who will pay for all this?"

"Oh don't worry about it, Mr Durtnall. I am sure there will be many volunteers who would love to help so as to get their village into the local news. The connection to the exhumation of Richard the third in Leicester will probably help get national news agencies involved. A lot of the analysis can be carried out using equipment in the office where this forensic anthropologist works. In fact, his firm might take this job on themselves as the trust officer in the museum said they were very interested!"

It was getting dark and chilly so they all started to pack up to go home. Tom said he would rebuild the church wall the next day before he returned to Oxford. Mr Hastings would keep in touch to let everybody know what was happening. He did caution everybody not to feel too excited yet. It was early days. The small bone fragments could be animal. Further searches might not provide anything else. Also, the church community had to be persuaded to let more intensive digging continue.

As Liam, Alyssa and their father were getting into Tom's van, Mr Hastings came over and asked to speak to Alyssa. "Could I just have a few words with Alyssa before you go? It is in connection with her homework?"

Oh, God! This is what I was dreading, she thought. They both walked a few yards away. "Mr Hastings, I have not given you any history homework." She thought it might be about something she said about the article in the Leicester Chronicle regarding the burial on Breedon on the Hill. She was right!

"Well, Alyssa you did ask me to get you some information for your history project in the holidays. Do you remember?"

She nodded her head.

"The article I sent you, described a traveller taking the dead children and their granny in a cart out of Ratby, but no mention was made to Breedon on the Hill. It did not mention the arrangements made to pick up the donkey that would have been tethered to the church gate. I have searched for other articles about this but there are none in the archives. So how did you know the exact place where the digging started so as to prepare for the burial?"

"I was dreaming a lot about travellers, Romany's. I must have dreamt it. Maybe a lucky guess? Oh and Tom Loveridge told me about the donkey being tethered to the church fence." Alyssa smiled sweetly at the teacher and ran back to the van. Driving off, she glanced back at Mr Hastings who was standing with a look of disbelief on his face.

"Hey sis." Liam poked Alyssa in the ribs. "I think when I grow up I want to be a phonetic antropolist!"

O Pisica De Familie
(A Family Cat)

It seemed to the children that September went very quickly as they became used to their new classes and teachers, some were starting their first term at the school. Liam thought his new teacher was hilarious. A chubby little man who always wore tweed style sports jackets and very bright spotty cravats. He thought he looked like a character out of a Charles Dickens Novel.

Mr Hastings had helped Alyssa finish the article for the local paper and then went on to make a booklet explaining some of the traveller heritage. Liam was kept busy providing sketches of Vardo vans and carthorses. He also had sketches of the cat and Tom and Gene Loveridge. When shown these sketches they were delighted so he had a few photocopied for other family members. He also drew the cottage at the back of the field. Finding this quite difficult as it had brought back strange memories of when he was there before in 1841. He had to stop a couple of times as the vivid images of him travelling through time made him feel quite feverish. But he then whispered, "Shut the door," to make the thought go away. He even put in his flier when searching for Snickitylickers. The family visited the church on some of the weekends as there was now a team of archaeologists working on the church site. They were volunteers and had found more human bones some of which were scattered over a wide area. The graves could have been plundered by animals that would have spread the remains further. Part of a headstone was found buried deep and the words 'Here lies P…' The archaeologists thought this could have been the headstone erected by the villagers who had collected money for the burial of the Romany family. The grandmother's name was 'Pat'. By mid-October, there was enough evidence to show there were three bodies, one adult female and two children, within the correct time frame. One half preserved jawbone of a female they thought could have been 'granny pat'. It seemed to be a close enough fit to show that a hedge burial had taken place on the hill in the 1800s.

Tom Loveridge considered this to be enough evidence for him to continue his work on renovating the old Reading Wagon. He also made a small casket for the bones which would be put into the van before it was burnt. He was still determined to have a traditional Romany funeral. John Hastings was still trying to persuade him to preserve it for future generations. Every time they met, they seemed to bicker at each other about it.

"Look, John don't start an argument again." Tom knew that look on his face and determination in his eyes to save the van.

"Tom, I just think you are letting down and hindering the development of the Romany culture. This wagon would be a 'showstopper' just remember the look on Liam's and Alyssa's face when they first saw it and that was before you started on the renovation."

"If you want a wagon like this,' build one 'yerself', lad now, 'taci'. In other words…" Tom zipped his lips with his finger and walked off.

There was also the problem of claiming the remains and removing them from a burial site. As the bones were found just outside the church, they could claim they were part of a planned burial. But who owned the bones? It seemed to be the church as they were found on church ground. Then there was the evidence from the forensic anthropologist team that the bones were from a Romany burial in 1800. Tom Loveridge became angrier the more this was discussed so John Harding said he would sort everything out. He was tempted to add only if Tom did not burn the Reading Wagon!

Snickitylickers had now adopted the Durtnall family. On returning home from Breedon on the Hill in September, the cat was sitting on their drive. Much to everybody's amusement, the cat followed the family in through the front door and had stayed with them since. Jenny Durtnall had asked the neighbours if anybody knew who owned the cat without success. Liam grumbled that this was not necessary as it was not long ago he had put his 'fliers' about the cat out in the village. The cat seemed to share her time between sleeping in either Liam or Alyssa's room. If they were watching TV she would often jump up and sit with them. Her favourite DVD was Mr Pompidou! This was played so much by the children Jenny complained she would be waking up in the morning with the theme tune of Mr Pompidou in her head!

The cat acted like a good alarm clock in getting the children up in time for school every morning. It saved James having to continually shout at Liam to get him to come down to breakfast before leaving for school. The cat would jump on

Liam's bed and sit on his head until he was wide awake. She would then do the same to Alyssa. This was a much calmer way to start the day and James who always took the children to school said it made the journey much calmer.

So the whole family spoiled Snickitylickers. Her favourite main meal was 'Ocean Recipes, little chunks of fish in a creamy sauce. Liam had tasted it as a dare and said he liked it as well. She also liked the chicken and cheese gourmet dish. Her favourite toy was a rolling ball cat teaser. She entertained the family for many hours playing with this. Jenny complained the animal was a time waster stopping her from preparing her lessons for the next day. Alyssa bought her a lead and used to take her out for walks around the village, or she was put in the car at weekends when the family went to Bradley Park. The cat would follow them. She would often disappear but always returned just as they were preparing to go home.

"I really don't understand how she does that," said James scratching his head.

"She certainly is a surprising little thing," Jenny replied. Jenny would sometimes take her into school for the day. The cat was very good with those pupils whose behaviour was a problem. She would often jump up onto the lap of a child who had been in trouble or had a fight in the playground and this would calm the child down in order for the teacher to discuss the problem later in the day.

Immormantare (Funeral)

Finally, as Allhallows eve approached the children became very excited. Tom Loveridge eventually was able to claim the human remains and they were now in the special casket he had made for them. In a traditional Romany burial, everything owned by the deceased would have been put in the caravan with the coffin. As there was no evidence of items like kitchen utensils, crockery or Jewellery. The Loveridge family had put in some trophies of 'best in breed' horses which were in the old wagon before the renovation. Awarded from competitions and gymkhanas in the past. Alyssa wanted to put in a picture of the parakeets they saw on their visits but the Loveridges when questioned had no knowledge of parakeets being kept by their ancestors. Alyssa decided not to say anything more about it.

Percy Taplet was also an excited man. The church council had signs made giving a potted history of the role the travelling community played when attending the protest marches against the Corn Laws in 1841. The local TV Company was setting up its cameras ready to film the occasion. Crowd barriers had been erected so as to make the area safe for onlookers. Everything was going to plan.

"Oh my, praise the lord for this bit of luck," the vicar shouted seeing some of his parishioners, the early birds who were setting a claim to the best places to view the funeral procession.

"Good morning, Miss Yates, hope the children have got over the food poisoning? How's Arthur has he now gone back to work at the bakers?"

Miss Yates scowled at the vicar not wanting others to know she was an unmarried mother and her husband who owned the bakery had gone down with food poisoning. This would not be good for trade.

"Ah, Mrs Muffin how are the piles, my dear? Did you try aloe vera juice? If it works for me, it should for you, eh? Bottoms up, I say." He laughed. "Oh, there's Mr Cox. Hi there, young man!" The vicar turned to speak to the crowd. "Do you know this man is an atheist? I have tried and tried to bring him into our Christian nest. But no luck, I am afraid. Can anybody help out here?"

Mr Cox glared at the vicar. His head seemed to shrink into his body as he hunched his shoulders in an effort to remain inconspicuous. There was a squeal from the crowd as Ms Burbridle a stick spindled young lady wearing a scarf and woolly hat, looking like a brown tea cosy. A passionate Christian. She rattled around the side of the crowd trying to get as near to this unfortunate young man who was on the verge of escaping over the hills and far away.

Back in Groby, the Durtnall family were in the BMW sport. James Durtnall's car and the only car the cat would travel in. She refused to travel in his wife's car. the Skoda Yeti crossover hatchback, Liam thought it had something to do with the name. The cat sat purring between Alyssa and Liam in the back seat.

"Hey, Snickity are you making yourself beautiful for the funeral?" Alyssa scratched the cat's head which made Snickitylickers purr even louder.

Liam reached across to tickle the cat's chin. "So when we get there Snickitylickers keep away from the Reading Wagon as we don't want you to get burnt."

There was quite a crowd in the village with the press and TV cameras. The whole place was buzzing with expectation. Vicar Taplet was rushing about all over the place. His arms outstretched flapping them like a wild goose. Trying to shepherd onlookers away from the church and into the designated viewing areas.

Liam and Alyssa when getting out of the car and seeing this collapsed in a heap of giggles. "Oh, look at the vicar!" screamed Liam.

Alyssa suddenly pointed up the hill. "There's his wife over there. She has just grabbed him by his habit and is pulling him away. I think he is doing more harm than good."

Signage had been erected showing information of Romany burials. They were dotted around the area outside the church. Large colourful displays erected on wooden panels. They had been weatherproofed and firmly attached to the ground by metal stakes. They ranged from those describing burial arrangements to the different makes of the wagon. Photos of the Reading Wagon which was the one being used for the funeral, were displayed together with other makes like the Brush and Ledge wagons, and the Bow Top, a lighter van and less likely to be turned over in strong winds. The logo of the Quarry was stamped on each sign as they had helped sponsor the event. Stalls had been erected selling models of wagons having been made out of matchsticks. Kits were available with instructions and templates to use so you could build your own wagon out of plywood. These being run by travellers wanting to make a profit.

"Roll up roll up ladies and gents to get a full working model wagon only a tenner today, buy now as they will go up in price tomorrow," shouted a rustic thin gentleman with a colourful tie, wearing a red shirt with a blue-collar and battered leather jacket with one button missing. A black mop of wiry hair that looked as if he had never put a comb through it made him look like a well-tanned Muppet.

Down at the bottom of the hill were a few tents erected by fortune tellers. They had not been allowed near the church so had set up camp by the roadsides. This was an illegal activity as they did not have license to trade on a public road. The local authority however was not making arrests as they did not want any trouble breaking out to spoil the day. The women dressed in flowing red and yellow dresses with mauve and green headscarves. Often with flowers pinned into their hair. Most wore very large gold earrings. Liam was fascinated by them and kept pestering his dad to let him have his fortune told. After rushing down the hill to enter one of the tents he came out with his eyes looking like saucers. "Wow, this lady was sitting behind a table with a huge glass ball, it seemed to change colour, and there were playing cards there as well," he said. "Dad, Dad, what does this mean? Can I have my fortune told? Can I find out what I will be doing when I grow up?"

James Durtnall was getting a bit cross at Liam's persistence and did not like his sleeve being tugged so as to get his attention. "Look Liam, can we concentrate on the funeral today. Maybe another time to talk about your fortune!"

"Pants, this is pants." Liam scowled and walked off.

Word had spread of this event and modern caravans used by the traveller community were parked at the bottom of the hill and on the surrounding roads. There was police traffic patrol officer's busy directing traffic through the village.

"I must check how much the church authority is charging stallholders?" muttered Tom.

"They are not charging them, Tom," John Hastings replied. "Vicar Taplet is in a generous mood this morning, he has just been given a substantial donation towards a new church roof. He told me that Christmas has come early!"

"Ladies and gentlemen, boys and girls, and of course travellers." Vicar Taplet had grabbed the microphone and was standing outside the front entrance to his church. The two loudspeakers erected on each side of the entrance, looked like dark coffins. They were huge and seemed to dominate the whole area. They were pushing out his message loudly and with a slight echo that made it sound a bit like a wailing ghost. Very appropriate for All Hallows Eve. "I welcome you to our Christian Church and am very glad to have you all with us to celebrate the history of our community. You will all be witnessing a Romany burial on behalf of the traveller community and to celebrate the bravery of those travellers who supported the protest marches against the Corn Laws carried out in Ratby in 1841. We now know those slain by that horse and cart were given a simple burial very near this church all those years ago. I like to think this being a link between our Christian ways and that of the Romany People. You all will be experiencing something never seen in North West Leicester before. I would ask you to remain silent once the funeral procession has started which will be in another ten minutes. At the bottom of the hill, you will see a Reading Vardo Van which contains the remains we think of the deceased that were given a shallow grave all those years ago. The Van will be pulled by two Irish Cobb horses up to the spot where the remains were found. In true Romany style, they will be cremated there. The burial up here that took place in 1841 is known as a hedge burial. This type of burial did not burn the deceased or their vans, unlike a traditional burial. The Romany community would carry out these types of burials when they were far from their home, and it would not have been practical to take the deceased back to their home town. The place of burial was only made known to the close family so that nobody would visit the site and steal the deceased possessions. Please do not embarrass the traveller community by asking them about the true place of burial. I invite you all to take some refreshment on the village green. There will be sandwiches and cake and thanks must go to the women's institute in Breedon for this. Please come along afterwards for a chat. There are also some pamphlets you can take home giving a 'potted history' of our beautiful church and lists showing the times of church services throughout the year. There is a short service tomorrow morning at 10.30 to celebrate 'All Saints Day'." There was a humming sound followed by a loud 'clunk' as the microphone was switched off.

"Ha the vicar did well, there, kushti, he knows a bit about our history," said Tom.

"Yes, despite him being eccentric, I think he is a bit autistic. But he is a serious historian. Did you notice the references in his speech to the Christian Church? I expect this was to make clear those telling fortunes down at the bottom of the hill has nothing to do with this ceremony! He also mentioned the 'All Saints Day' mass tomorrow!" said John Harrington.

Tom started laughing. "Even so I should think he might have upset some of his parishioners! Oh, I see that the Wagon has arrived." As he saw the wagon being lowered off the truck that had parked at the bottom of the hill. He called out to Gene to come with him and they both set off down the hill. They would be driving the Wagon together and Gene would be taking off the harnesses to lead the horses away once they got to the church. Tom turned around and went over to Liam and Alyssa. "Come on then you two. There's room for both of you at the front of the wagon, can you can squeeze in with Gene and me!"

Both children stared at each other. Jenny Dartnall laughed. "We all wanted to surprise you both so we did not tell you before, but you have worked so hard on this project you both deserve to be leading the procession in the van!"

Alyssa and Liam just stared at each other. "Wow, this is something we will remember for the rest of our lives," Alyssa gasped.

Liam with a shout of joy had already run over to the wagon and was scrambling up into the driver's seat. Alyssa and Liam felt quite important and this reminded them of when the news of this first was made public at school.

"Hey, Liam we are the stars again!"

Liam giggled, memories of his failed attempt to get his fortune told quickly disappearing.

The crowd of onlookers seemed to raise their heads at the same time as a faint jangling sound heralded the arrival of the Reading Van pulled by the Irish Cobb horses. People were leaning forward and pointing down the hill. The Durtnall family with John Hastings had the best viewing spot with the Vicar and his wife. Decking had been used to make a platform above where the crowd was standing and the area had been roped off.

As the two horses started the ascent. Tom had borrowed them from a friend who managed to hire out Vardo wagons to holidaymakers and he also supplied the horses. The Cobb horses had been trained to pull Vardo Wagons. These horses would not stop until they reached the top of the hill. If they did stop they would never be able to pull the heavy wagon from a stationary position. Their massive shoulders with long mains in black and white looked like scarves hanging down from their shoulders. They had strong muscular necks with broad chests with 'white feathered lower legs that could be seen faintly blowing in the breeze. Their small but determined faces always alert and concentrating on the task with strong hind legs. The odd twitch of an ear showed how alert these horses were to the crowds that were standing at the hillside. They seemed to glide up the hill using a strong but steady gait. Tom gently flicking the whip just above their heads so as to help them keep to that steady rhythm. It was quite a rocky ride and Liam was holding tightly to Alyssa to stop himself from falling off into the crowd. The Reading Wagon looked immaculate. An ivory-coloured roof with ruby red sidewall with the intricate carvings of woodland creatures, squirrels and wild plants. Everything was gilded and shiny with cut glass used in the skylights in the roof. The horses were now on level ground and were led around to the back of the church. Tom stopped the wagon over quite a large bonfire that was ready to light. Gene jumped off the wagon and took some time to take off the harnesses before the horses were taken away. By now Vicar Taplet had put on the CD Tom had given him. The Mediaeval Babes. When They Turuf Is Thy Tour. A soft mournful wilting melody seemed to crawl out of the loudspeakers and spread like treacle through the air.

"Liam, this is the song we found on that piece of parchment in the cottage," whispered Alyssa. "It is a sad creepy song and it makes me want to cry."

"Well, it is about death and the lack of any sort of feeling the dead have in their other existence! What do you expect?" Liam snorted.

The horses had been led off to a place of safety. The crowd; expectant. All eyes focussed upon Tom who had got off the van and had opened the door of the wagon. The two children jumped down and stayed close to Tom. He then ambled over to a lighted taper being held by one of the other travellers standing by the church. The music started again. How Death Comes. The final track on the CD. In contrast with the last song. This was a raucous chant slamming out into the gathering dusk making both Alyssa and Liam jump. This was raw, robotic. Full of hate, some of the younger children in the crowd were upset and were being taken away by their parents. Liam and Alyssa just gritted their teeth. "This reminds me of when we saw the cart at Ratby in 1841. The anger of the crowd when they saw the accident caused by the constables

on the village green. Tom has chosen the music very well."
Alyssa sighed.

Tom with the burning taper in his hand, lit two more and gave each one to the children. "Alyssa, go around to the back of the van and place your taper under the rear wheel, Liam, you do the same," as he started to light the bonfire under the front of the van. It had been dosed with petrol and there was a small deep explosion more like a puffing sound as the tinder was set alight. Tom then threw the remains of the taper into the caravan and stood back. There was a groan from John Harding. "What a waste."

Alyssa and Liam threw their tapers underneath the back of the van and ran over to Tom who guided them back away from the van to a place of safety. Alyssa looked up at Mr Harding. He had tears in his eyes.

There was a disturbance in the crowd. Fingers started pointing as a cat was seen running up to the blazing Reading Wagon. Red fire from within blistering the ornate gilt on the outside walls as the smoke turned black swirling like a large oily snake wanting to escape from the top of the roof.

"Alyssa," screamed Liam in a panic getting ready to rush out to the wagon. "Look, that cat is Snickitylickers."

It was as if Alyssa had been given an electric shock. She screamed and both children started to run to the van. Tom quickly grabbed both of them. "Tom, stop the cat please, Tom," shouted Alyssa, but now the crowd was getting excited and with the bangs and crackling from the wagon, Tom did not seem to hear her. However, he did see the cat.

"Alyssa!" Liam shouted. "It will be OK, Tom will stop her from entering the wagon!"

But instead of trying to stop the cat, Tom did just the opposite. He stood aside and watched as Snickitylickers ran straight past him, mounted the steps to the front of the wagon and dived into the fiery furnace. Liam with tears running down his cheeks started kicking and punching him. "Why did you not stop her?"

Alyssa dragged her brother away. She was frightened that Liam would try and go into the wagon after the cat. There were screams and shouts from the crowd nearest the wagon as they could see what had happened.

Tom hugged Liam with a sad smile on his face. "Liam," he said gently, "Snickitylickers was the Georgio, she was the family pet and would have wanted to go with the remains. She had to go with them. She was with them in 1841, my son."

Liam said nothing, just stood too near the fire quietly sobbing. Alyssa put her arms around him, she looked up at Tom. "Why did she have to die, Tom?"

"All animals and pets would have been put down anyway see." Tom gave each child a hug and walked back to meet Gene to take the horses back to his friend.

All the family were too upset to stay long for the wake. On return home, the first thing they saw was Snickitylickers' bowl standing forlornly in the kitchen. Her collar with Snickitylickers written on the side was curled up inside it. "How did that get there?" said Jenny.

It seemed a funny thing to do but they all sat down in the kitchen just staring at the bowl. James Durtnall was the first one to speak. "I had a word with Tom before we left as we are family. He has invited us to help with scattering the ashes back where the family was living in 1841. Remember, Snickitylickers' ashes will be there as well."

"So where is this James?" asked Jenny Durtnall.

Alyssa jumped up from her chair. "It will be the cottage, won't it? That's where they were living!"

"Clever girl, Alyssa, but we must not tell anyone and we cannot have any plaque made in the cottage as it still is rented out in the holiday season," said Tom.

"But we can have pictures of Snickitylickers, Dad."

"Yes, Liam we can!" This seemed to cheer Liam up. He got up and took the bowl and the collar.

"Good! The bell still works. I think we could get these made into something useful?"

"Yes, let's work on this together, Liam." Smiled Alyssa. "I know we could put one of your sketches of her from the wanted poster you did a couple of weeks ago and stick it onto the bowl."

"Or I could do another smaller picture?" said Liam. Both children ran off into the lounge full of ideas. James and Jenny Durtnall smiled at each other.

"I think things will be OK!" said James.

Machka Cat

The next morning and the beginning of the weekend, both children were out early going to see Toby who lived in the next village. He was very good at photography. His dad being a professional photographer who had a studio in Leicester City. They were going to have a photograph taken of Liam's new sketch of the cat, the feeding bowl and the collar. The idea would then be to have a plaque made up in memory of Snickitylickers where they would keep it in the house. Further conversations with Tom and Gene who said they could bring the plaque over to the cottage every Halloween if they wanted to have a small ceremony of remembrance. As they were continuing to walk down the street deep in conversation Liam heard a tinkling sound. He grabbed Alyssa by the arm and they both turned around to see what they thought was a Siamese cat.

"No, I don't believe what I am seeing!" gasped Liam.

The travelling community has a rich heritage that is not understood by many. 77% of Roma and Travellers have experienced hate speech or hate crime. 50% have experienced discrimination in the workplace, 70% have experienced prejudice in education. The more information readily available to the public can only be good things in helping others understand a culture that is different to their own. A regular source of information is through the Travellers Times www.travellerstimes.org.uk. These are often available in local libraries.

If you enjoyed this book…

Thank you for reading this book, if you enjoyed it I'd be grateful if you could leave a short review on the book's Amazon page.

Amazon.com | Amazon.com.uk

I would be very interested to hear your thoughts on the story. This helps me when writing the next two books in the series. 'The Cottage of Conjurations and Strife' where the children travel back in time to Fishmonger row in London and meet the Witchfinder General. The third book 'Family', where they are taken into the future to a world being taken over by developing 'mind control' technologies.

Thank you for your help,

R.I.Tapley